P9-CFN-592

SOMETHING UPSTAIRS

AVI

SCHOLASTIC INC.
New York Toronto London Auckland
Sydney Mexico City New Delhi Hong Kong

FOR R.J.

No part of this publication may be reproduced, stored in a retrieval system, or transmitted in any form or by any means, electronic, mechanical, photocopying, recording, or otherwise, without written permission of the publisher. For information regarding permission, write to Scholastic Inc., Attention: Permissions Department, 557 Broadway, New York, NY 10012.

This book was originally published in hardcover by Orchard Books in 1988.

ISBN 978-0-545-21491-9

12 11 10 9 8   11 12 13 14 15/0

Printed in the U.S.A.   40
This edition first printing, July 2010

Those who cannot remember the past
are condemned to relive it.
Santayana

AUTHOR'S EXPLANATION

This is the strangest story I've ever heard.

Since I write books for young people I often visit schools. It's good to get out of my writing room and into the world where my readers live. Besides, I like kids.

During these visits it's not unusual for grown-ups as well as kids to tell me stories about their lives, stories they think will make good books. Even if I don't get ideas to write about, at least I have a chance to meet some interesting people.

One day, on just such an occasion, in Providence, Rhode Island, a teacher took me aside.

"I have a boy who's very anxious to meet you," she said. She acted as if it were a secret.

"I hope you can fit him into the schedule," I

said politely. Inwardly, I groaned. The day was already too full.

"He insists on a private meeting."

"I'm really not sure . . ."

"He's read all your books."

"All?" I said doubtfully.

"All," she insisted. "He's got it into his head that you're the only one who can understand him."

I have to admit I was flattered. And curious. I murmured a "Well, maybe . . ."

The teacher gave my arm a squeeze. "Wonderful," she said. "You could take part of your lunchtime . . ." Off she ran before I could tell her I'd rather have all my lunch.

It was not to be. Halfway through my meal I felt a tap on my shoulder.

"Avi?" It was the teacher, with a boy in tow. "This is Kenny Huldorf," she said. "Kenny, this is Avi."

There was nothing unusual about Kenny Huldorf, not at first sight. He was on the small side perhaps, but there was every indication that he was about to double his size any moment. His hair was short and light. A few childlike freckles splashed his cheeks. And he must have been pulled from gym, because his face was red and his shirt untucked.

"Hello, Kenny," I said and held out my hand.

He took it and gave it a tentative shake. There was a stare too. It's a look I've seen many times, and I can never tell if it's awe or disappointment.

"I've got a quiet room for your talk," the teacher informed us.

Reluctantly, I got up. In moments we were closeted in a small room, and before I could say a word she was gone, the door firmly closed.

Feeling trapped, but knowing there was nothing I could do about it, I motioned Kenny to one of the two chairs.

He sat down. I sat down. We looked at each other. The truth is, I think neither of us felt the other was very promising, though *he* was the nervous one. From his pocket he drew out a key chain and started to fiddle with it. I decided it was up to me to begin. "I understand you wanted to speak to me," I offered.

"I've read all your books," he got out, still playing with the chain.

"Hope you enjoyed them."

He nodded, then said, "Did you do all that stuff in your books?"

3

"Hardly any," I told him. "Writing is mostly imagination, emotion, things you've noticed or heard about rather than things you've done. . . . Why don't you put that chain away? It's distracting."

A frightened look came into his eyes. But it passed quickly and he seemed to take hold of himself. Then he said, "What about memory?"

"Memory?"

"You know, in your books, was any of that stuff . . . things that happened before?"

"I just said, almost none of it."

He looked at me searchingly. "No, what I mean is, is any of it part of someone else's memory?"

I gazed at him, baffled and more and more uncomfortable. All I could manage was a change of subject. "What was it about my books that caught your interest?"

"They made me feel you'd understand something that happened to me."

"Oh?"

He shrugged, indicating frustration. "I've tried to tell people. But they don't want to hear."

"Why not?"

"Too weird."

I sat there, wishing I had never offered to listen. But I could see no way out without hurting his feelings. "Okay," I said, settling back into the hard wood chair, "try me."

"Really?"

"That's what you wanted, isn't it?"

"Yeah . . ."

I glanced at my watch. "Kenny," I said, "if you don't start, we're going to run out of time. Now put your chain away and tell me what's on your mind."

With that he took a deep breath, shoved the key chain into his pocket, and began.

* * *

It was, as I said, the strangest story I've ever heard. Not only did I listen then, but I spent the afternoon after school listening. And the evening. What's more, I stayed over at a local hotel a second day to check out what he'd told me — at least those aspects that were possible to check.

When I was done I offered to write it all down as a book. With what I took to be great relief, Kenny Huldorf agreed.

* * *

This is it. His story. My writing. I think it's true.

CHAPTER ONE

As far as Kenny Huldorf was concerned, Los Angeles, California, was perfect. All his life he had lived in nothing but spring and summer weather. It never rained. The sidewalk trees were oranges and lemons. There were flowers on every street. When he planned to do something outside, he could do it, even a beach picnic on Christmas day — a Huldorf family tradition.

Kenny could, and did, play baseball most days. True-blue fan that he was, he carried a good luck Dodgers key chain in his pocket wherever he went. So when Kenny's parents announced that they had taken new jobs and had already bought a house across the country, in Providence, Rhode Island, he was not happy. He wasn't even sure he knew where Rhode Island was, other than near the Atlantic Ocean, three thousand miles from the Pacific.

He checked an atlas and discovered that the state — the smallest in the Union — is so small that the city of Los Angeles couldn't be fit into it. "Little Rhodey" people call it.

Rhode Island, he learned, calls itself "The Ocean State." Its motto is "Hope." But hopeful was not what Kenny felt. On the day he was informed they were moving — the last week in *April* — it snowed in Providence. Kenny had seen snow on mountain peaks, but only from a distance.

Kenny finished his school year. The family packed. They drove east. And it was mid-August when they rolled off the interstate. His father took three left turns and there they were: Sheldon Street. Their new neighborhood.

"Welcome to Providence," his mother announced.

What Kenny saw that day was as different from Los Angeles as he could imagine. The street was narrow, crowded, and old. The air was muggy. No majestic palms or sweet-scented orange blossoms cheered the senses, only a few skimpy trees and old-fashioned lamp posts.

Though a few buildings were brick, most were wooden. Many had plaques which bore odd names and dates from long ago.

"When the houses were built," his mother explained.

"There's ours," his father said, pointing across the way to number fifteen.

Kenny looked. It was a broad, cream-colored, three-story building with wooden siding, shuttered windows, and a high-pitched roof covered with shingles. A central door painted dark brown stood above a couple of stone steps which rose from the narrow brick sidewalk. There was a plaque on it which read:

DANIEL STILLWELL HOUSE
BUILT 1789

Inside was a central hallway and a steep flight of steps. On each side were the main rooms, rather small.

Kenny drifted from room to room, downstairs and up. The movers hadn't arrived so there was nothing in any of them. And yet, he remembers having the distinct sensation that the house was *not* empty.

"What do you think?" his mother asked.

"It's okay," Kenny told her, trying to sort out his feelings. "Which is going to be my room?"

"We had an idea," his father said. "Follow me." He headed for the kitchen and a door Kenny had not noticed. It led to a narrow flight of steps that corkscrewed up two flights. Kenny followed his father. His mother followed him.

At the top they came into a long, open attic. There were two low windows that hugged the floor, ceiling beams above, a floor freshly sanded and oiled. A new bathroom. The whole area was bright but hot, with stale air.

"How's this?" his mother began. She was smiling broadly.

Kenny looked around. "For me?" he asked.

His father, grinning too, nodded to the question.

"Really?" said Kenny. For the first time since he entered the house he felt like smiling. What he saw was more space than he'd ever had, both private and special.

His mother went on. "It hasn't been lived in for years. We did it completely over. If you want it, it's yours."

"It does get cooler," his father added. He

10

reached toward a skylight and pulled a pole. Opened wide, the skylight seemed to gulp like a gasping mouth. The air began to cool.

Kenny walked the length of the attic, thinking of ways he could fix it up.

"If you'd prefer," his father offered, "you can have one of the downstairs bedrooms."

"I'll take this," Kenny said.

At the far end of the attic he came upon two doors. He pulled one open and looked in. It was a small room, no more than nine feet by twelve, the ceiling steeply pitched. Too big for a closet but hardly big enough for much else.

His father looked over his shoulder. "Must have been where the servants lived," he suggested.

"It's so tiny," Kenny said.

"The good old days . . ."

"Those are the original floors," his mother told him. "And walls. Mr. Bosco, the inspector who checked the house for us, got excited when he saw them."

Kenny said, "Looks dirty."

His mother laughed. "Think *original*," she said.

Kenny pulled open the second door and peered in. It was a smaller room than the first, dingy, hot, with a harsh, musty smell. There were no windows. Yellowing paper hung from the walls like the skins of tired bananas. A dark stain covered the center of the floor.

When Kenny stepped in, he felt an immediate sense of unease. And the next moment he thought he heard a faint rustling sound. He turned, expecting it to be one of his parents. Neither one was there.

"Dad?" he called. "Mom?"

"Going down!" came a shout from the stairwell.

Certain he'd heard something, Kenny turned back into the small room. The stain on the floor caught his eye again. As he looked at it, the thought came to him that it had something to do with a human death.

And with that thought came a sensation of shame, as if he, in some way, bore some responsibility.

He shook his head and the moment was gone. He was fine. And the stain was just that, a stain.

*   *   *

A new city. A new house. Unopened boxes piled high. On most of the windows no curtains. Things to sort and put away. Endless fixing up to do. Rooms to paint. No time to do any of it. . . . And the heat was high, a record drought hot enough to bring sweat just with breathing. TV weathermen were speaking ominously of no letup, and they were right. The streets were deserted as people huddled around their air conditioners.

Kenny remembers being bored. Restless. Edgy. He kept trying hard to find a place for himself, but without much success. His parents had started working immediately, and since he had no friends and school was still weeks off, he spent most of his days alone. This gave him time — more time than he wanted — to wander about. What he discovered was that Providence was not an ordinary city.

There were stone posts on curbs for tying up horses, blocks to mount for climbing into carriages. There were cobblestones in courtyards, and curious names on plaques, names such as Esek Ormsbee and Peleg Quimby. Two streets from his house was a building two hundred and fifty years old. Older than the Revolution. Older than the French and Indian War.

The Huldorfs' new home was one of the old buildings. In fact, after they moved in, their real estate agent brought them a scrapbook which provided the history of the house and the land on which it sat — information from 1636 up to the present. Maps, deeds, and, for recent times, photographs of the area, things that helped Kenny visualize the place as it had been.

Though he had never been particularly interested in history, Kenny now felt an urge to know about the old days. More than once he asked himself, Who were the people of this house? What did they look like? Did they wear funny suits, wigs, dresses? Were there any kids? How did they live? And, for that matter — how did they die?

*   *   *

What Kenny recalls is that a few nights after they moved in the heat had become so awful it was particularly hard for him to fall asleep. And then when he did, a mosquito awakened him. At least Kenny thought it was a mosquito.

Half awake, he fumbled for his bedside flashlight and shined it at his clock. It read two-thirty-five A.M. He looked about. Though the attic corners were still caught in darkness, enough moonlight seeped through the open skylight to give the room a soft yellow glow, thick and hazy.

He tried to settle himself, to find a cool spot on his pillow. But he kept thinking about something his father had said, that servants once lived in the small rooms off the attic. How could they have stood it on such a hot night?

He heard a sound. His first notion was that it was an owl. Or a bat. He lay still, listening hard.

It came again. He describes it as a scraping sound, the kind of noise you'd make if you put light sandpaper to wood and rubbed slowly.

Sitting up now, Kenny tried to pinpoint where the sound had come from, using his bedside flashlight to probe the corners. He couldn't see a thing. Perhaps he had imagined it.

Determined to sleep, he flopped down, only to hear the sound once more. This time he was certain it came from the far end of the attic — where the small rooms were.

Taking up the flashlight, Kenny slipped out of bed. . . . A mouse didn't bother him. He wasn't too sure about a rat. That thought made him snatch up a shoe as well and hold it by the toe, hammer fashion.

Kenny crept forward as quietly as possible, stopping every couple of feet. Sometimes he heard the soft scraping. Sometimes he didn't. It was, he thought, the sound of something being pushed or dragged along the floor.

He reached the first of the doors, but instead of barging in, he waited. He wanted to make sure he had the right room, afraid that if he went into the wrong one, he'd scare off whatever was making the sound.

After a while, when no sound came, he tucked the flashlight under his arm, reached for the doorknob, and twisted it, carefully pulling the door open. Clutching the flashlight again, he leaned forward and looked.

Light from the single window fell upon a couple of cartons his parents had stored inside. That was all that he could see. He switched on the flashlight, but saw nothing else. Still, Kenny waited, hoping the sound would come again. When it did, it came from the other, smaller room. Kenny turned off the flashlight, drew breath, moved to that door, pulled it open, and cautiously looked in.

A white glow, almost shiny, and brightest on the floor, filled the windowless space. And what Kenny saw — or thought he saw — were two hands, then two arms, reaching up from the stain, pushing away a box of his mother's old books that was sitting on it. These hands and arms seemed to be not flesh and blood but sculptured, glowing smoke. It was as if, from under that box, a body was struggling to be free.

Astonished, Kenny stood staring, telling himself that what he was seeing was not real. A dream perhaps. Some kind of fancy. But no, not real.

Bit by bit, the arms edged the box off the stain. It seemed like hard work. Their muscles bulged with effort. Sometimes, as if tired, the arms would seem to rest. Then the hands with their small but perfect fingers would curl around the box's edge flexing out apparent pain.

It took an hour for the carton to be pushed away. Kenny watched it all. When the job was done the hands reached from the floor, held onto the box, and . . . pulled.

A head rose from the stain. Then came a neck. Then shoulders. The rest of the body. Soon the whole thing stood upon the floor — still and waiting. A soft, pale, pulsing glow radiated from its body, a glow which formed a vague boundary

17

between air and mass, in equal parts nothing and something.

Except it was clearly not a *thing*. It was a shape like a human being.

The figure had no shoes. But Kenny recollects seeing trousers and a shirt, not tucked in, whose frayed sleeves reached midway between elbows and wrists. A stain was spread upon the back of the shirt.

The more Kenny looked, the more certain he was that this was a boy.

As Kenny watched, the boy approached the far wall, where he began to feel about its surface, as if he were in search of something, as if he were looking for a way out.

He tried the second wall. The third.

Kenny fumbled for the flashlight switch and turned it on, aiming it right at the form. The light went through him. He cast no shadow.

Just then Kenny saw, with a mixture of thrill and horror, that the boy was about to move toward the door wall. They would come face to face.

The figure turned. Their eyes met. Unexpectedly, the boy's hand reached toward Kenny. Taken completely off guard, Kenny reacted defensively, lifting his shoe to protect himself. The boy shrank back as if expecting a blow. And the next second he vanished, leaving Kenny to stare into the empty room.

It was as if the boy feared *him*.

CHAPTER TWO

Kenny made his way back to bed, determined to think through all that had happened. But the next thing he remembers is the morning sun pouring through the skylight, waking him.

As soon as he realized it was morning, he jumped up and went to look at the room. All he found was that same small, empty, dirty, and very dull room. But the single box of books *was* pushed off the stain.

Gazing at the stain again, Kenny was reminded of his thought when he had first seen it: that it had something to do with a death. There was nothing about the stain itself to put him in mind of a person. Or death. Just a dark blotch. Then what, he wondered, had caused him to think that?

* * *

Kenny was glad to find his parents had not yet left for work.

"Any plans for today?" his mother asked him.

Kenny shook his head, slumped into a chair, swallowed some juice, and poured himself some cereal.

"Somebody told me about a swimming club," his mother went on. "I think you could walk to it. You'd probably meet some other kids too. Interested?"

"Sure," Kenny said.

"I'll try to get off a little early," his father said. "We could check it out then, or you can do it on your own."

"Where is it?" Kenny asked.

His father told him. Kenny had already learned enough of the area to realize it wasn't far. "I'll do it myself," he told them.

As his mother was about to take off, she gave him a kiss. "Sorry this time is such a drag," she said. "School will start soon."

"I'll live," he assured her.

"Good," she bantered, giving him her brightest smile. "I'd hate to see you otherwise."

Something about her words stirred him. "Ma!" he called, just as she reached the door.

She stopped.

"Do you," Kenny asked, "believe in ghosts?"

"Ghosts?" she said, surprised.

"Right. Ghosts."

His father looked up quizzically from behind his paper.

"What makes you ask?" she said.

"Just curious."

"No," she said, "I don't." With a wave and a smile she left.

Kenny's father gave a shake to his paper. "What made you ask that?" he wanted to know.

Kenny checked himself. It was hard to tell his father he believed the attic was haunted. "A dream I had," he managed. "About something upstairs."

His father laughed. "Hey, everybody has something upstairs."

Kenny looked up. "What do you mean?" he said.

"You know," his father said off-handedly, "something you don't want anyone to know about. Secrets."

"What about a ghost?" Kenny asked cautiously.

His father chuckled. "If anyplace has the right to a ghost," he said, "it's here."

"Why?" "Providence is a really old town. Lots of things must have happened here."

"Do *you* believe in ghosts?" Kenny asked him.

"Nope," his father replied and retreated behind the paper.

"Dad?"

"What?"

Kenny said, "You know that scrapbook we were given?"

"About our house?" His father lowered the paper. "Sure."

"Well, it has all these names in it. People who lived in this house. . . ."

"Right."

"How could I find out more about them?"

"Such as what?"

"Who they were. What they did for a living. If they had any kids who lived with them. Stuff like that." He tried to make it sound of no great consequence.

"You certainly are caught up in this place, aren't you?"

"I guess," Kenny said sheepishly.

"Glad you have something to occupy yourself," he said. "It makes me feel better about this time."

"What do you mean?"

"I don't know," he said. "Sometimes strange things happen to people in strange surroundings, particularly when they don't have much to do. So your project sounds worthwhile. You'll be our resident historian. I suppose a library could help you." He fetched a phone book and flipped through the pages. "There's one on Ives Street. Where's that?"

"Not far," Kenny said. "Walking distance."

*   *   *

After breakfast Kenny went up to his room and took out the scrapbook about their house. In it he studied the names of the people who had lived on their plot of land.

> Williams Family (1636–1743)
> Sheldon (1743–1769)
> Stillwell (1769–1845)
> Blaisdell (1845–1849)
> Lawton (1849–1867)
> Lake (1867–1890)
> Vickey (1890–1912)
> Butter (1912–1929)
> Myers (1929–1930)

Salazar (1930–1947)
Flood (1947–1963)
Melton (1963–1987)

Their street was named Sheldon. He made a connection there. As for the rest, the names meant nothing to him. He copied out the list and set off.

At the Ives Street branch library Kenny quickly located a few books about Providence.

For a small place, he discovered, the city has an enormous history. He learned about the person who founded it, Roger Williams; how Providence people argued among themselves, with Massachusetts, with Connecticut, as well as with the English king about becoming a colony; how Providence joined with the Island of Rhodes, to arrive at the official state name, "The State of Rhode Island and Providence Plantations." He learned that the first big American war — against Indians — ended in a massacre nearby. He read about the burning of the ship *Gaspee*, a prelude to the Revolution; about what happened in Providence during the Revolution; how the people of Rhode Island didn't approve of the Constitution because it was not democratic enough.

He found chapters about famous Providence sailors and merchants; how far they sailed; how they were the first Americans to go to China; how brave they were; how they grew rich trading rum and molasses. And, finally, he learned how some of them — full of democratic ideals for themselves — made great sums of money bringing back people from Africa and selling them in the South long after the slave trade was illegal. But Kenny could find nothing about his neighborhood, much less his house.

When he explained to the librarian what he was looking for, she said, "What you want is the Historical Library. That's exactly the kind of thing they specialize in. It's only seven blocks from here, where the streets called Hope and Power meet."

* * *

The historical library, one of the old buildings and not exactly cheerful, is a big, dark brown block of a place. Kenny had to ring a bell to get in, then he was questioned at the main desk.

"I need to do some research," Kenny told the librarian.

The man pushed forward a notebook and handed Kenny a pen. "Just sign in there, will you?"

Kenny signed. The man looked at the signature.

"Huldorf . . . Sounds familiar," he murmured, and pulled a card from a drawer. "Right. Just got a message this morning. Someone up in Administration is expecting you."

"Me?"

"Fifteen Sheldon Street?"

Kenny nodded.

"Yes, you'll have to check in the administration office for permission to use the collection."

"Where's that?"

"Go out into the hallway. Turn right. You'll see some steps. Go on up. When you get to the top, turn to your left. It'll be the first open door on the right. Got that?"

Puzzled that he should be expected, Kenny walked out into the deserted hall, made a right turn, went up the steps. At the top he had to stop and think over the directions before making

27

another right turn. There Kenny found an open door. He walked in.

The room he entered was shadowy except for a lemon-colored blade of sun slashing through a tall, coffin-shaped window at the end.

The walls were covered with shelves, and the shelves themselves were filled with yellowing papers, boxes, and books. The air was laden with dust.

In the middle of the room was an antique desk, and behind the desk a man in black. He was a small, thin man, white-haired. His fingers were narrow and long, with carefully trimmed nails.

At the front of his desk was a brass name-plate. It read:

PARDON WILLINGHAST
Historian

"Sir?" Kenny said finally. He had been stand-ing in front of the man for a few moments without being noticed.

The man looked up. His parchment-colored face, lined like a map of many roads, seemed rarely to have seen the light of day. His eyes were both dark and deep. His expression was grim. "May I help you?" he asked softly.

Kenny gave his name.

"Huldorf," the man said. "Ah yes." He drew himself up. "I believe your family has just bought and moved into fifteen Sheldon Street. Is that correct?"

"Yes, sir. How come you know?" Kenny asked.

The old man was silent for a moment. Then he cocked his head slightly to one side. "House transfers are listed in the newspaper," he said. "I have a desire to keep track of the old ones. It's a way of making myself useful — here at the library — to new owners who often show up."

Satisfied with this explanation, Kenny told Willinghast that he wanted to find out about the people who used to live in his house. "I've got a list," he said. "*Can* I find out some stuff? Use the library?"

"May I," asked Willinghast, "see the names you brought?"

Kenny offered the list. He remembers fiddling with his key chain while the man studied the paper.

Willinghast looked up at him at last. "Do you have any knowledge about these people?" he said.

Kenny shook his head.

"May I suggest that there won't be much about them," Willinghast said. "Not if this is all you have. If you will allow me, I'll retain it and check through some of my own resources. Come back tomorrow and I'll tell you what I've been able to find. Is that agreeable?"

Kenny said yes.

"Good," said the man. He rose and came out from behind his desk. "I'm always here. At your service."

With a gesture, Willinghast guided Kenny to the door.

*   *   *

Once more Kenny stood in his attic looking at the room, his eyes drawn again and again to the stain. Finally, he knelt by it. Touched it. It felt cold.

It was then that he had an idea. Using an old Boy Scout knife, he pried up a splinter of the wooden floor from the area of the stain and carefully wrapped it in a tissue.

After dumping his allowance savings into his

pocket, he took the splinter around the corner to Wickenden Street, where there is a pharmacy.

"Can I help you?" asked a white-coated woman behind the counter.

"It's sort of weird," Kenny said, suddenly feeling awkward.

"Give it a try," she said with a smile.

Kenny explained who he was, where he lived, that he and his family had just moved in. He said they were fixing the place up and wanted to paint some floors. But one floor had a stain on it. His folks, he said, needed to know what that stain was before painting.

"Is there any way to check this out?" He unrolled the tissue and handed the woman the splinter.

The pharmacist held it up, gave it a squint, and said, "Not that unusual a request. We can send it in for chemical analysis. It will cost."

"How much?"

"Oh, ten dollars. . . ."

Kenny counted his fistful of coins. Just barely enough.

The woman asked his name.

He gave it to her and asked, "How long will it take?"

"I'll call as soon as a report comes in," she replied.

Kenny thanked her and left.

*　　*　　*

It was during dinner that Kenny asked his parents, "Why do ghosts haunt houses?"

His father turned to his mother. "Kenny dreamed about ghosts last night."

"Oh, dear."

"First of all," his father continued, "I don't believe in ghosts, as I told you. Secondly, they supposedly haunt places because something awful happened to them there. You know, a person is killed and his ghost remains in the house. Or something unhappy occurred there. At least, I think that's the notion. I've never heard of a happy ghost. . . . Have you?" he asked his wife.

She shook her head. "That must have been a vivid dream, honey," she said.

"It's living in an old house, in an old city," his father put in. "Lots of memories here."

His mother said, "I don't believe in houses having ghosts." Then she added, "But, you know, I'm willing to admit they have memories."

It was a thought that intrigued Kenny. "What's the difference?" he asked.

His mother thought for a moment. Then she said, "I'm not sure."

It was then that Kenny — without saying anything to his parents — made up his mind. That night he would set his alarm for two-fifteen and try to see exactly what was happening in that room.

CHAPTER THREE

Kenny is certain that it wasn't the alarm that woke him, but sounds coming from the small room.

Heart pounding, he checked the clock. It was a little past two. Hastily he turned the alarm switch off and listened. Another sound came. It was the same he had heard before, an irregular scratching and scraping noise. A thought struck him: the ghost — if it was a ghost — *wanted* him to wake up.

Kenny slipped out of bed quickly but quietly and made his way across the attic. He had left the door to the little room slightly open. Taking a deep breath, he reached out to give it a tug. It swung open half an inch more, enough so he could look in.

The ghost-boy was already there, straining

upward from the glowing stain. Soon he stood in the middle of the room, his back to Kenny, glowing like smoldering, dark brown earth.

As he had done before, the ghost moved to the far wall, then felt its surface as though trying to find a way to escape. Gradually, he worked around the room until once more the two boys were facing each other.

This time the ghost's look showed no emotion. Certainly no inclination to speak. And although Kenny had the feeling that it was the ghost who had summoned him, he decided that if he wanted talk he'd have to start it.

"Who are you?" he whispered.

The ghost inclined his head a little. Kenny wasn't even certain he had heard. He said nothing, only shifted very slightly, as though he could hear better with one ear than the other.

Kenny tried again. "Please," he said. "If you can't tell me your name, I'd like to know *what* you are."

The ghost pointed down to the stain. Kenny's eyes followed the gesture. "I don't understand," he said. "Does the stain have something to do with you?"

At that point the ghost gave Kenny something like a nod. He even turned around, showing off the stain on his back.

"I'm not getting it," Kenny said. "Can't you talk?"

The ghost's mouth opened. He seemed to be trying to say something. It didn't come. He tried again. This time he managed to utter one sound and one alone. It was hollow, indistinct, as if he had forgotten how to speak.

"What?" Kenny said.

The ghost repeated the sound.

To Kenny, the sound, or word — he didn't know what it was — sounded like . . . *ave,* or perhaps . . . *save.* He repeated it to himself once, twice, three times. Suddenly it came. "Oh!" he blurted out. *"Slave!"*

The word, flung out so suddenly, seemed to strike the ghost with enormous power. He retreated to the farthest wall and lifted his arms as if to protect himself.

Kenny saw that he had said something terribly wrong. Wanting to apologize, but not knowing how, he took a step forward, reaching for the ghost-boy to reassure him. But to Kenny's dismay the ghost didn't understand the gesture. Instead, he cringed back and, like melting ice, sank into the floor, leaving the room dark and as empty as it had been before.

*　　*　　*

Next morning Kenny slept late, missing his parents at breakfast. When he finally came downstairs he found a note informing him when they would be home, and asking him please to call one of them at work.

But before he could call, the phone rang. He thought it would be his mother, but it was the pharmacist.

"The lab has identified what caused the stain," she told Kenny.

"Oh, right," he said. "What was it?"

"Blood. Human blood."

Kenny was not surprised. "From long ago?" he asked.

"Yes, exactly."

"How long?"

"More than a hundred years. Otherwise they would have to report it to the police."

"Any way to be more exact?"

"Apparently not."

*   *   *

After breakfast Kenny called his mother and told her he was going over to the Historical Library.

Willinghast was waiting for Kenny. He was pleased, he said, that he had returned. In his formal way, he told Kenny that he had some information — not much perhaps — but some — about the names on the list.

Kenny said, "I think I only care about the ones from more than a hundred years ago."

Willinghast looked up. "May I ask why?"

"They'd be the most interesting ones," Kenny said evasively.

Willinghast considered him carefully. Kenny insists the old man must have known he was not being completely candid.

After a moment Willinghast said, "Permit me to share with you the full extent of my investigation." He slid a paper over the desk. Next to each name a line of information had been provided.

Williams Family (1636–1743)
    Land used farming
Sheldon (1743–1769) Merchant

Stillwell (1769–1845) Chandler.
    House built in 1789
Blaisdell (1845–1849) Merchant.
    Went to California in gold rush
Lawton (1849–1867) Sea captain
Lake (1867–1890) Banker
Vickey (1890–1912) Merchant
Butter (1912–1929) Lawyer
Myers (1929–1930) Baker
Salazar (1930–1947) Carpenter
Flood (1947–1963) Professor
Melton (1963–1987) Veterinarian

Kenny studied the names and the information. "Can you tell which ones might have had slaves?" he asked.

Willinghast gave him an intense look. "Slaves?" he said, speaking the word with disdain.

"I mean," Kenny said, "do you think any of them owned slaves?"

"It is possible."

"When did they outlaw slavery?" Kenny asked.

"You are asking about Rhode Island, I presume."

"Yes."

Willinghast sat back. "No more slaves," he began, "were to be brought into the state after 1774. In 1784, a new law was passed. Those who had been slaves remained so, while their children born after that time remained slaves only until they reached the age of twenty-one. It was a most liberal position.

"Of course eventually, all slavery was prohibited by amendment of the Federal Constitution."

"But before that," said Kenny, trying to remember references he'd read, "wasn't slavery very important to the state?"

"The trade brought riches to some," Willinghast allowed.

"Weren't there people," Kenny continued, "who wanted to get rid of slavery?"

"There are always those," the old man agreed, "who desire to rush history."

"What do you mean?"

"Oh," said Willinghast vaguely, "agitators and the like. May I inquire as to why you are so interested in the subject?"

Kenny replied, "Just ... am. Could kids be slaves?"

"I believe I just informed you about that."

"Well, how can I find out which of those people on that list had a kid for a slave?"

"I have serious doubts that you can. More to the point, I assure you, it's not worth the bother."

Kenny looked over the paper again. It gave him too much information and too little all at once. He didn't know what to make of it or where to begin. He tried another approach. "What," he said, "about murders?"

"Murders?" said Willinghast. Some color came into his pale cheeks. His eyes were fixed on Kenny.

"If someone got murdered," Kenny continued blithely, "would it be in, say, newspapers? I mean, they didn't have TV or radio, or anything like that. But, you know what I'm saying, would it have been reported?'"

"Is it a slave who might have been murdered that has caught your interest?"

"I think so."

Willinghast shook his head. "Hardly likely that such a thing would have been reported."

"Why?"

Willinghast shrugged. "It was not considered important."

"How come?"

The man made an open gesture with his hand. "My boy, we are talking about slaves." He spoke as if the word explained his meaning. "Trust my judgment. It is not something I would worry about. If I were you I should cease your search."

*　　*　　*

When the ghost-boy appeared that night Kenny, still dressed, was waiting, standing in the dark by the door to the small room.

Kenny watched, fascinated, as the ghost heaved himself free of the glowing floor, like a swimmer coming out of the water after a long pull, grabbing the end of a dock, hauling himself to shore.

Once up, the ghost approached the far wall and, as before, began to search it.

Kenny said, "Are you looking for a way out?" He had made up his mind to speak softly, not wanting to alarm the boy as he had done the night before.

The ghost stopped and turned, bestowing on Kenny a clear gaze of contempt. Then he continued his search.

Kenny decided to say nothing else, waiting instead for him to make his way around the room until they would face one another again.

Sure enough, when the ghost came to Kenny's side of the room he paused. His look, unmistakably angry now, was baffling to Kenny. But the pause did allow him to notice more about the figure: the scar on his left cheek, and the fact that, though the ghost was shorter than he, he appeared to be older.

"I think I should tell you," Kenny said, "I'm living here now. We just moved into the house."

Those words made the ghost's eyes narrow slightly. He backed up a step.

Emboldened, Kenny went on. "You were a slave," he said. "Is that what you meant to say when I asked you yesterday?"

The ghost considered him carefully. Then he said, "I am a . . ." He didn't finish.

"A *what*?" Kenny coaxed.

"A . . . slave."

'You mean, you *were* a slave."

The ghost shook his head. "No, now."

"I don't understand."

The ghost pointed down.

"Blood," Kenny said.

To which the ghost added, "Mine." And he returned to exploring the walls with increased urgency.

"You don't have to do that," Kenny suggested. "The door is open. You can see that, can't you? I mean, I won't prevent you from leaving or anything like that."

The ghost halted his search and looked at Kenny with intense suspicion. But then he did turn to the door.

Kenny backed out of the way. "Come on," he urged.

The ghost shook his head. "I cannot."

"Why?"

"It is forbidden."

"By whom?"

"I am a slave."

"There *are* no more slaves," Kenny said. "All that stuff's done with. They outlawed it."

Again the ghost shook his head. "A ghost is but a memory of what once was." And again he approached the walls.

Kenny decided it would be better to change the subject. "What's your name?" he said.

No answer.

"Mine is Kenny. Kenny Huldorf. I'd really like to know yours."

The ghost stopped his searching and looked over his shoulder. "Why?" he asked.

"You know . . . to be your . . . friend."

"Friend," said the ghost, almost spitting out the word.

"Really, you can trust me. Come on. Just tell me your name."

For a moment the ghost stared at Kenny. Then he said, "Caleb," and turned back to the wall.

Kenny watched him a while, trying to find a way to ask the question he wanted most to ask. "Caleb?" he said at last.

The ghost turned to face him.

"Did you really . . . get . . . killed?"

"Yes."

"Here? In this room?"

"Yes."

"Was it . . . an accident?"

"No."

"Did someone . . . murder you?"

"Yes."

"Who?"

"I do not know."

"How come?"

"I was asleep."

Kenny swallowed hard. His mouth felt dry. *"Asleep?"* he managed to say.

The ghost nodded.

"Do you know *why* you were killed?"

"To keep me a slave."

Kenny, who was feeling increasingly upset, said, "Can you tell me more?"

"They were making trouble for blacks."

"Who were?"

"People."

"Why?"

"We wanted to be free."

"And?"

"I tried to prevent them. When I did I . . . think . . . they killed me."

"You said, 'think.' Does that mean you're not sure?"

"No, I am not sure." Caleb turned back to the wall.

Kenny said, "Well . . . can I . . . you know . . . help you in some way?"

Caleb swung back around to face Kenny. He seemed incredulous. "You?" he said.

"Honest. I want to help."

Caleb, with even more intensity, studied Kenny. Then he said, "Perhaps."

"Great. Just tell me how," Kenny insisted. "I'll try. Honest."

The ghost continued to stare, as though

46

trying to judge Kenny's words. Finally he said, "Help me . . ."

"Go on. . . ."

"Help me find my murderer."

Kenny had a distinct feeling of shock. "That's impossible," he protested. "It must have happened a long time ago."

"And that is something which you know nothing about, do you?"

"I've read some things."

"Read," said Caleb scornfully.

"But . . ."

"Learn for yourself," Caleb said with growing anger. He pointed to the door, started to say something, but abruptly turned and once more began to search the walls.

After a moment, Kenny said, "Caleb? Can I ask you some other stuff?"

The ghost paused only long enough to say, "Leave me."

Kenny, not sure how he'd offended the ghost, waited in hope that he would say more. When he didn't, when it was clear that he really was very angry, Kenny stepped into his own room. But it had completely changed.

CHAPTER FOUR

The room was shabby and dirty, heavy with heat. None of the things which Kenny called his own remained. Even the painted walls and skylight were gone. Baffled, he turned toward the small room, hoping Caleb would give him some explanation. But Caleb still had his back to him.

Wondering if other things — even outside — had changed, Kenny went to one of the windows and looked down. On a stoop across the dark street a man was standing, gazing straight at Kenny's window. Kenny drew back, then crept forward to look again.

The man was wearing what appeared to be a long black cape which reached his knees and a hat, triangular in shape. Its brim obscured his face.

As if suddenly realizing he was being observed, the man began to descend hurriedly from the stoop into the shadows. He moved so quickly that he stumbled, missed a step and almost fell. The next moment he sprang up and, keeping his face averted, fled up the street.

Kenny's first impulse was to tell Caleb, feeling instinctively that there must be some connection between him, this man, and what had happened to his room. But though he knew the ghost remained in the small room he decided not to say anything. Caleb's abrupt dismissal still hurt. He made up his mind to find out more on his own.

In a rush now, Kenny bolted down the steps. At the first floor landing he quickly unlocked the back door, then tore around to the front of the house. The man was nowhere in sight.

Kenny looked toward Traverse Street. A few people were about, but no one resembling his man. He turned toward Benefit. A figure in a dark cape was just going around the bend. Kenny took off after him and reached the corner in moments. By then the man had almost reached Transit Street.

"Sir!" Kenny called.

Instead of responding, the man made a sharp turn down the street's steep incline. Kenny ran after him, trying to avoid bumping into passersby. At the corner of Benefit and Transit, he paused and looked down the hill, certain that was where the man had gone. But something was wrong. For that time of night there were too many people out. And they were oddly dressed. Women's skirts were long. Men wore capes or coats with tails. Three-cornered hats were everywhere.

Kenny glanced at the sky. He was certain it was close to three in the morning. It shouldn't be so bright.

His gaze shifted to the bottom of Transit Street. Instead of seeing the Interstate highway, he had an unobstructed view of the Providence River, very much wider than he remembered it.

He looked up. The Electric Company building and smoke stacks which usually blotted out the southwestern sky had disappeared.

As for the river — Kenny took in the view with something close to amazement — it was crowded with sailing ships.

Kenny made his way down Transit Street, across South Main, and then to the river's edge.

Thoughts of the man with the cape were gone. Instead, he stood where he was, absorbed in the astonishing sight.

For Kenny found himself looking over a scene thick with wooden wharfs, and with more ships than he could count, big as well as small, their masts and spars like so many porcupine quills gone mad. Loose and lumpish sails hung fluttering in the light breeze. And there were miles of rope supporting all this rigging and sail, enough to make him think of a gigantic spider web flung across the sky.

Around these ships, in them, on them, great numbers of men were working. Wearing trousers and shirts of soiled canvas, they were hauling, lifting, shoving bales, boxes, and kegs over wood, brick, and stone. Most used their backs to do the work. Others used carts or wagons pulled by horses, and a few by oxen.

From all about came a hubbub of shouting, hammering, even singing — noises punctuated by the neighing of horses, the crack of whips, the barking of dogs, the ceaseless cry of sea gulls swooping above.

Across the wide street from dockside stretched a long row of wooden or brick buildings. A few were stone. Some, it was easy to see, were dwellings; others looked like cafés or taverns. But there were many more buildings which appeared to be warehouses. Kenny could see goods being hauled to second-story widows by rope and pulley.

Over all, the air was ripe with the stench of salt, sweat and fish, tar and horses. Things rotting, things alive. To Kenny's eyes the whole scene was a confused swirl, a vision of constant energy. But as he stood there — Kenny was emphatic on this point when he told his story — he understood what it was he was seeing. All about him lay Providence as it *had* been. He was seeing the past. And he was in it.

He was, quite understandably, shocked and fascinated. Questions of why and how quickly gave way to a bursting desire to see more. Pressing forward he made his way through the crowd, but no one paid him any attention. This puzzled him at first. After all, he knew very well he was from the twenty-first century. Then he looked down at himself and realized that his clothing was different. He was barefoot. He wore trousers and a loose-fitting shirt. When he ran his hand through his hair he found it was longer than usual.

Suddenly nervous, he reached into his pocket and felt for his key chain. As he closed his fingers around it, the connection to his own time calmed him.

Leaving the waterside, Kenny made his way through crowds to the largest of the market buildings. Built of brick, it was three stories high, with the lower level open. Men dressed in the style of the Revolutionary War were standing around piles of goods, bargaining with one another, bickering, occasionally breaking into boisterous laughter.

Just outside the building, one man in particular caught Kenny's attention. He was an elderly man, large, dressed plainly in a frock coat and a broad-brimmed hat. His hair hung down loosely over his shoulders. He was in the midst of a heated discussion with another, smaller man.

Curious, Kenny drew closer.

"They were stout enough to fight thy battles in the late war," he heard the large man say.

To this the other replied, "They aren't to be trusted. If you push your views so, it will disrupt the principal business of this community. This is all agitation."

"Agitation!" the large man cried. "I tell thee

53

slavery is a piece of evil as sure as I make my mark here!" From his coat he pulled out a large key and with powerful strokes used it to cut an X in the brick wall of the building. "As long as that remains," he said, "I shall never change my mind. Nothing shall stop me from supporting their demands." With that, the man brushed past Kenny and stormed off.

"Mr. Brown!" cried the other. But the man called Brown was gone.

As Kenny watched, the smaller man peered at the mark on the brick and shook his head. Then he turned around.

"You there, boy!" he snapped.

"Me?" said Kenny, taken by surprise.

"Yes, you. Step this way."

Not knowing what else to do, Kenny approached him.

The man took a folded scrap of paper from a pocket and thrust it at Kenny.

"I shall be much obliged to you if you would take this to number eighty-four Benefit," he snapped. "No need to wait for an answer." And without waiting himself, the man hurried away.

Kenny looked at the folded note. The name "Seagrave" was scrawled on it. After a moment's thought Kenny decided to complete the errand. He wanted to learn more about the world he had entered.

Walking casually, taking in the sights, he made his way up the steep hill which he knew to be Thomas Street, until he reached Benefit. There he searched out the number.

Once he saw the house he stopped and looked at the piece of paper in his hand. His curiosity was too great. After a glance around to make sure he wasn't being observed, he stepped into a little alley, unfolded the paper, and read what had been scrawled. Kenny remembers it quite well. It read:

W says he is Ready to act. He has His man. As Brown and his Faction Will not listen to Reason I believe he is right. Meet on the morrow, evening, nine, The Gaspee, to Plan.

O.

Disappointed that the note provided so little information, Kenny went to the door of number eighty-four and knocked.

A young woman with a white cap on her head opened the door partway and looked out.

"Yes?" she inquired.

"A message for Mr. Seagrave," Kenny said. He offered the note, hoping to learn more about the business from her.

But without a word the young woman took the paper and shut the door. Clearly, she saw him as a boy of her own time, a messenger of no consequence.

It was this lack of notice that prompted a frightening thought. Had he, he asked himself, been cut off from his real home and *his* own time? Was he stuck in the past? Just the idea made his heart beat fast.

The next moment Kenny was tearing down the length of Benefit Street. At Sheldon he stopped, breathless, afraid to look at his house, afraid not to. But when he did look, it was there, exactly where it was supposed to be.

With a gasp of panic he realized that it was painted quite another color than he knew. And the shutters were not there. Nor was there any historical plaque. At that point Kenny realized he was seeing his house not as it was in the twenty-first century, but long before. He was still in the past.

His panic growing, he charged across the

street to the side of the house where the family car normally sat. It was nowhere in sight. But the back door was. He yanked it open and tore up the staircase to the attic. By the time he reached the top he was struggling for breath. He forced himself to look. It was as he knew it. He had returned to his own time.

Although enormously relieved, Kenny was now as much confused as to why he had come back to the present as he had been about finding himself in the past. How had it all happened? The only answer he could think of was that it had to do with Caleb, that the man on the street as well as the past itself had been summoned by Caleb somehow.

Kenny remembers rushing into the small room, hoping the ghost would still be there. He was gone.

Unable to answer the question, and suddenly weary, Kenny stripped off his clothes and climbed into bed. There he pulled the sheet up over his head and closed his eyes.

As he lay there he felt a momentary but overwhelming sense of confusion. Was he in the present, or the past — or both at the same time? The next thing he knew it was morning.

CHAPTER FIVE

Kenny didn't get up right away. He didn't want to. Too much had happened during the night. Too much was whirling through his mind. He kept telling himself that everything he'd experienced was a dream, a mixture of all the pictures he'd seen, the history he'd read, his imaginings about old Providence.

Yet he was absolutely certain he had smelled a different air, felt a different ground beneath his feet.

Then he thought over the conversation with Caleb. Caleb *was* a ghost. By that time Kenny had no doubts about it. And Caleb's words had been very clear: he had been a slave and had been murdered. Caleb said there was a connection between the two, being a slave and being killed.

Finally he had asked Kenny to find his murderer.

But how could he find a murderer from almost two hundred years ago? It *had* to be a dream. Kenny closed his eyes again. It was much easier to retreat into sleep.

When he finally rolled over to look at the clock it was eleven-thirty in the morning. And the phone was ringing in his parents' room on the second floor. It was his father.

"Kenny?" he said. "You were supposed to call me."

"Sorry. I just woke up."

"Just now?"

"Yeah." His father's voice relaxed. "You must have been tired."

"Guess so."

"You were up in the middle of the night, weren't you?"

"What do you mean?"

"I think I heard you coming up the steps."

"You did?"

"If I remember right — I was pretty sleepy — it must have been around three. Were you getting something to eat?"

Kenny was relieved his father had supplied an excuse. "Right. Got hungry."

"Glad that's all it was. Any plans for today?"

"I think I'll go over to the library. Then get in a swim."

"Sounds good. Interested in going to a ball game tonight?"

"Boston?"

"Nope. Pawtucket. Just north of Providence."

"Who's playing?"

"People call them the Pawsocks. It's a triple-A team. Might be fun. Be like looking into the future."

"What?"

"You never know. Maybe some of the players will turn into stars. Then you'll be able to say, I saw those guys when . . ."

"Sure . . ."

"Okay. I'll be home no later than five. We'll grab a bite, then go."

Kenny put the phone down. It wasn't the ball-game he was thinking about. Or stars of the future. The fact that his father had heard him on the steps was proof that at least some of what had happened the night before was no dream.

Kenny almost picked up the phone and called his father back, feeling a great desire to tell him everything. Instead, he decided he had best check on some things first.

He dressed and went outside. For a moment he just stood, looking up and down Sheldon Street. Then he set off, following the same route he had taken the night before through old Providence.

He walked slowly, feeling a mixture of tension and excitement. What he saw was all so much the same. And all so different.

At eighty-four Benefit Kenny studied the house to which he had delivered the note. There was a plaque on it which read:

PHILIP SEAGRAVE HOUSE
BUILT 1792

Along the waterfront hardly a trace of what he had seen the night before was in evidence. The river was narrower, and large sections were covered over. One building was pretty much the same, though: the market he had visited the night before. What's more, the plaque on it indicated that it *was* an important site a long time ago, having been rebuilt in 1797.

As Kenny looked at its windows he recalled the large man he had seen, who at the end of his argument had cut a mark in the brick.

At that moment it occurred to Kenny that if what he had seen was real — not a dream — he might be able to find that mark.

He attempted to position himself where he'd stood the night before. Then he tried — in his memory this time — to see what he had seen then. Finally he began to search the bricks, first by looking, and when that didn't work, by feeling. It took a while, but he found it. The mark was about four and a half feet above the ground, not very distinct, but unmistakable: an X cut into the brick, which he had seen being made almost two hundred years ago!

For the rest of the day Kenny was in something of a daze. He kept going over all that had happened, trying to make sense of it. He could not. As a result he never called his father.

*   *   *

"You enjoying this?"

Kenny assured his father that he was. If he'd been taken to a ballgame a month before — even a minor league game — he says he would have been ecstatic. Now as he watched the Pawtucket Red Sox play the Toledo Mud Hens, it took effort to keep his mind on which side was up. He felt as if the game was going on forever. And he had a different kind of forever on his mind.

That night when Caleb emerged, Kenny was waiting for him again by the open door of the small room.

As he had done each time before, Caleb paid no attention to him at first, but put his hands to the walls.

"What do you keep looking for?" Kenny asked.

"A way out," Caleb replied.

"Why can't you just walk out this door?"

At first Caleb merely glared at him. Then, like a teacher tired of explaining something obvious, he said, "If a person dies in an unnatural or unjust way, that person's memory stays fixed in time and space."

"Is that what you are, a memory?"

"Yes."

"And you stay that way, forever?"

"Some memories fade. Others are forgotten. The bitter ones become ghosts in search of an altered past."

"Can memories change?"

Caleb looked at Kenny suspiciously. "Why do you want to know?" he asked.

"I told you. I want to help."

The ghost sneered, "So you say."

"I mean it!" Kenny protested.

Caleb seemed to relent a bit. "If the circumstances of the unnatural death are altered, then the memory can change."

Kenny shook his head. "I'm not following you."

"I was killed," Caleb said with rising anger. "I am a prisoner, here, of that memory."

"Murdered, you said. . . ."

"If I knew who murdered me," Caleb continued, "I might be able to prevent it from happening and thus be free to leave this place."

Kenny nodded. "So you want me to do two things," he said. "First, find who your murderer was. Then, help you keep him from killing you."

Caleb nodded. "To free myself both things are needed," he said and began to search the walls again.

To the ghost's back, Kenny said, "And you're not saying keep you from being killed *now* . . . but *then*. When it happened. Right? Years ago."

"Of course," Caleb said as if what he was suggesting was perfectly normal.

After a moment, Kenny said, "When I left you last night I went outside. It was still Providence, but Providence from a long time ago. In your day, I think."

Caleb stopped his wall search and looked at Kenny. Kenny thinks he remembers just the touch of a smile on the ghost's lips. "Is that the truth?" he said.

Kenny nodded. "I only went because I saw someone standing outside looking up here."

"*This* house?"

"I wish you'd believe me," Kenny pleaded. "Some man was looking up at my window. I saw him right after I spoke to you."

"What did he look like?"

"I couldn't tell. But he looked suspicious, so I ran after him. I couldn't catch up. Could *you* go out into that past?" Kenny asked.

Caleb seemed to stand a little taller. "You would have to lead me," he said.

"If I did," Kenny said quickly, "you'd have to tell me what to do. I mean, I don't know anything about how it was then."

"I'm not surprised," Caleb said sarcastically.

"Why?"

"How many white boys care about the memory of a black?"

Kenny felt stung. "I have to ask you something else. There was another man. It was down by the marketplace. He asked me to deliver a note."

"Can you describe him?"

Kenny did the best he could.

"Esek Ormsbee!" Caleb cried. "A slave merchant. To whom did you deliver the note?"

"Someone named Seagrave."

"Another slaver."

"Before I delivered the note," Kenny said, a little embarrassed at the admission, "I read it."

"What did it say?"

Kenny repeated the words as he remembered them. "Has it anything to do with your being killed?" he asked.

"They are planning a disturbance in the black district. That man you saw outside this house must have been part of it too."

"Are you sure?"

"If Ormsbee was there, and if that was the message, then it is happening again."

"What do you mean? What's happening?" Kenny said.

"They are trying to provoke an incident. After that will come my murder."

"I don't understand."

"Why should you? It doesn't concern you, does it? It happened a long time ago," he added, echoing words that Kenny had used.

"Caleb," Kenny protested, "I just moved here. I don't know anything about this!"

"You went out into the past," Caleb reminded him. "My past *before* my death, when they were planning my murder."

"I don't even understand how it happened," Kenny said.

"You entered someone's memory."

"Whose?"

"It may be mine," said Caleb.

"Or . . . it may be that person you saw."

Kenny was unnerved at the thought. "What do you mean?" he cried. "Who else could it be?"

"I don't know."

"Is there any way of discovering?"

"Go out again."

But the notion that someone else — someone he didn't know — was controlling events was too frightening. Kenny thought of the man who had been watching his window, the one he had tried to follow and couldn't. "I'm not going," he said with a nervous shake of his head. "Once was enough."

"But if *I* can get there," cried Caleb, "then *I* can try to prevent what happened. Prevent it and I shall be free! Don't you see? I cannot leave this room myself. I am a slave even in death. Someone has to lead me into my own time. You said you wanted to help me. Did you mean it?"

Kenny had the sense to understand the danger. What if he couldn't get himself back to the present? Avoiding Caleb's eyes, he said, "I'll make up my mind tomorrow."

Caleb gazed at him. Once more Kenny felt in the look an undisguised contempt. "Yes," the ghost said. "It would take much courage."

*   *   *

By the time morning came, Kenny knew that he needed to talk to someone. What Caleb was suggesting he do was too scary. Worse, he felt Caleb was now *demanding* that he go into the past a second time to help him. He was still not clear how it was even possible.

Once more he thought of talking to his parents. But so far he had left them out of it completely —

and not just because they were busy. He kept feeling they wouldn't believe him. What would convince them? A visit with Caleb? But Caleb seemed so angry. . . . What if Caleb objected to seeing them? Or, worse, what if they upset him so much they frightened him away forever? Or kept Kenny away from Caleb so he couldn't help? At that moment Kenny didn't want to change any of that.

* * *

"Can you tell me," he asked when the ghost appeared that night, "the date you were murdered?"

"What difference does that make?" Caleb demanded.

"You said you didn't know what happened, right?" Kenny answered. "Maybe there was some report about it. I mean, a report might even say who your killer was."

"It is not likely," Caleb said.

"Worth a chance, isn't it?"

"You are trying to avoid helping me," the ghost said sharply.

"No, really . . ." Kenny said, ashamed to admit it, though he knew it was true.

"The white boy offers to help the black boy," Caleb said sarcastically. "The black boy accepts. But then, the white boy becomes fearful. You don't believe what I have told you, do you?" Caleb sad, his voice shaking.

Kenny was torn between guilt and fearfulness. "I *do* want to help you," he insisted. "Only . . . only it seems . . . dangerous."

"Yes, it is."

"Well, maybe," Kenny tried, "maybe I can help you without going back to your time. Know what I'm saying? It would be safer."

"For whom?" said Caleb, making no attempt to hide the scorn in his voice, and forcing Kenny to turn away from his accusing eyes. But then, after a moment he said simply, "The last day I can recall is August 17, 1800."

"Is that the day you were killed?"

"I do not know. Dates of the year were not important to me," he replied.

"Why?"

"A slave," he reminded Kenny, "does not possess his own time. Not even that."

"August 1800," Kenny said. "I'm going to check something tomorrow."

"*Then* will you make up your mind?"

Kenny said, "I promise."

Caleb drew himself up. "I have experienced the promises of white people," he said.

"Caleb, I'm different," Kenny insisted.

"We shall see," Caleb returned.

*　　*　　*

The newspaper room in the historical library was large, with high, dark ceilings from which a few fans hung. They stirred the heavy, hot air lazily.

"May I help you?" asked a young woman from behind a desk.

Kenny explained, "I'd like to look at some Providence newspapers from around August 1800."

"I can't let you look at the original papers," she told him. "But I can set you up on microfilm. Would that help?"

"Okay. Thanks," Kenny said. He had used microfilm for school projects back in California.

The woman led him into a small room, to a row of microfilm reading machines. Lined up they looked a bit like large computer screens. No one else was working there.

"You can sit here," the woman said as she left the room. In a few moments she returned with a small spool of film in her hand. She set the film up on the machine.

On the screen Kenny saw the page of a newspaper with tight, narrow columns, no headlines as he knew them, nor, for that matter, any pictures. He had to lean close to read the words.

"Just work this crank," the woman explained. "It turns the pages. You can pick up the date here."

She pointed to the side of the screen. "Call me if you have any questions, or when you're done."

Kenny turned the crank slowly. Most of the stories seemed to be about the comings and goings of ships. He did find one article about the revolution in France. There was also one about the Presidential election contest between Thomas Jefferson and John Adams.

But he hardly thought he would find news about Caleb's death on the front pages. He spent most of the time looking at the back where there were obituary lists.

In the issue of August 27, 1800, Kenny found what he was looking for. It was tucked between an ad for a shipload of molasses and news about a proposed canal. It read:

CURIOUS DEATH

The death of a slave named Caleb, aged
about Sixteen — property of Daniel
Stillwell — discovered on August 18th.
The boy was found in his own Room,
the door being Locked. Authorities can
provide no knowledge of the Events, and
surmise, in Consideration of the Facts
that, since the Door was locked from
the Inside, the boy took his own life.
Mr. Stillwell, the boy's owner, was away,
and knew nothing of the Matter.

"Find what you want?" asked the librarian
when Kenny returned the film.

"I'm not sure. . . ." he said.

She took the box and smiled. "Next time if
you come, it would probably be good to stop off
in the administration office first and get permission. Just a formality."

"I did," Kenny told her. "Mr. Willinghast said
I could."

"I'm new here," she said. "I don't think I've
met him yet."

"Oh, well, thanks."

*   *   *

Kenny said it was his mention of Willinghast that made him think he should inform the historian of his find. As before, Willinghast was in his office behind his desk, sitting silently among the room's crisscross of shadows. Without being asked Kenny sat down in a chair.

Willinghast looked up. "I believe you have found something," he said.

"How did you know?" Kenny said, taken by surprise.

"You have a look of perplexity."

Kenny said, "Didn't you tell me it would be hard to find something in the newspapers — the old newspapers — about Caleb's death?"

"Caleb?" Willinghast said, looking slightly amused.

Kenny realized that he hadn't told Mr. Willinghast about his meetings with Caleb. And wasn't about to. "That's the name of the slave who died in my house," he explained. "I found it in the papers."

"Historical research is often the beneficiary of luck," Willinghast said dryly. "Pray tell me, what else did you find?"

"This slave, Caleb, the one who died in our house, probably committed suicide."

"Did he? How unfortunate!"

"They knew that because they found him in his room," Kenny went on, "and the room was locked. From the inside."

"I see. . . ." said Willinghast. His eyes, alive with interest, were steady upon Kenny.

"What do you think?" Kenny asked.

Willinghast said, "Since you have elected to come this far, perhaps there is a need for you to pursue the matter farther." He allowed himself a thin smile. "It is said young people enjoy mysteries."

Not sure what to do or how much to say, Kenny sat quietly for a moment, toying with his key chain. When he looked up, Willinghast was gazing at him steadfastly.

"I better go," Kenny said, standing. Willinghast sat back. Kenny recalls his saying, "I look forward to seeing you again."

CHAPTER SIX

When Caleb returned that night he fairly sprang out of the floor. "Have you made up your mind?" he demanded.

Kenny shied from the question. "You know," he said, "that date you gave me — the last time you remember being alive?"

"Yes?"

"I looked it up in an old newspaper. At the Historical Library." He was watching Caleb carefully, wanting to gauge his reaction. "You were found, here, in this room, on August 18, 1800. The newspaper report said you killed yourself."

"That is a *lie*!" Caleb shouted.

"The report said the door — that door — was locked from the *inside*."

"I was murdered!" Caleb insisted.

"What about the door?"

"I do not care about the door," Caleb said. "How do *you* explain the blood on my back?" He swung about so Kenny could see the stain again. "Do you believe I could have shot myself there?"

Kenny had to admit it wasn't likely.

"Of course," continued Caleb, "they would say I took my own life. Far better to announce that a slave — some miserable black — killed himself, than to confess their own crime. Who would care besides other blacks? It is my belief that I was killed to give my brothers and sisters a message."

"But," Kenny persisted, "if the door was really locked from the *inside* how else would it have happened?"

With an impatient gesture, Caleb waved Kenny's question aside.

"Anyway," said Kenny, "there's another thing. If you were a slave, what about your owner?"

"Mr. Daniel Stillwell."

"Where was he?"

"He and his whole family went down to Newport."

"Why didn't they take you?"

"I was to watch the house."

"Then you were in the house alone."

"All these questions!" exploded Caleb. "You will not trust me, will you?'"

"Do you trust me?" Kenny retorted.

"No!" Caleb said, turning from him. Then, in a gruff voice, he said, "It was Mr. Stillwell who ordered me to stay up here. You see," he added, "I am not allowed to go down into their rooms." He turned back again to Kenny. "Believe me, if I knew who killed me I could explain all these things you ask. And this is what I want you to do: help me learn what happened."

"I understand that. But . . ."

Caleb drew himself up. "Maybe *you* have no reason to care about my murder. I do. Now, are you going to help me or not?"

Kenny looked at Caleb. There was a kind of fury coming from him that was as desperate as it was fierce. And then, quite suddenly, Caleb's whole tone shifted. "All I ask," he cried, "is that you trust *me*. I was a slave all my life. In my memory — which, as I stand here before you now is what I am — I am *still* a slave. You can help me change that. I implore you, do so while there is the opportunity!"

The pain in Caleb's words cut Kenny's last defenses. As though it were a voice separate from his own, he heard himself say, "I will."

Caleb took a deep breath and squared his shoulders. "Give me your hand," he said.

After a moment of hesitation Kenny reached toward him. And he has a distinct memory of their hands meeting. He saw that. He insists he felt nothing, no more than if he'd held his fingers to the air. But gradually Caleb did take on weight, form, and warmth, until their hands — hands of flesh and blood — were linked.

"Now," Caleb said, "lead me out of this room."

Kenny backed through the doorway. As soon as they crossed the threshold, Caleb released his grip and stepped away into the middle of the attic room, which again had become what it once was. Turning slowly, cautiously, he moved his arms and hands as if testing the air.

Kenny is certain that the stain on his back was gone, as was the scar on his face.

Caleb went to the top of the steps. There he paused. "When we walk the streets I shall stay one step behind you."

"I'd rather be together," said Kenny.

Caleb shook his head. "This is not your memory," he said. "It is mine. Be warned, you must do as *I* tell you."

Kenny started to protest, but thought better of it. At the same time he reached into his pocket and touched his key chain.

Caleb started down.

*   *   *

It was dark outside, but Sheldon Street was busy, the air sultry. Soon sweat trickled along Kenny's back and down beneath his arms. His clothes, heavy and coarse, didn't help.

When the two boys moved to Benefit and then to Main, they found more people. Many of them seemed to know one another; there was much stopping and talking. Kenny was fascinated by the way they looked and would have liked to listen to their conversations, but Caleb, a step behind, kept urging him on.

The dock area looked very different from when Kenny had seen it before. Under the dark and heavy heat, all was still. Ships on the river rose and fell, creaking and groaning with the swollen tide. Sails hung limply. Workmen sat about with shirts off, seeking any feather of breeze. Kenny could see the smoldering embers of their pipes glowing like cat's eyes. The gulls were still.

Sensing tension in the air, Kenny stopped. "What's the matter?" he asked Caleb.

"Come on," Caleb said evasively. "We must not be late."

Across from the wharfs stood a number of low buildings from which lights blazed.

"Grog houses," Caleb explained. "We want that one." He was pointing to a tavern whose sign bore a crude picture of a sailing ship in flames. "The Burning Boat."

Kenny remembered his reading of Rhode Island history. "The *Gaspee*," he said. Caleb nodded. Outside, men and even a few boys sat about on benches drinking.

As Kenny and Caleb drew closer the men eyed them suspiciously.

Kenny stole a quick, anxious glance at Caleb, but Caleb's face revealed nothing of his thoughts. His voice low, he told Kenny simply, "Inside."

There the foul air was layered with drifting sheets of stale tobacco smoke. Men sat about tables, their glistening faces bathed in pools of candlelight as they drank, played cards, or just talked. The babble of voices made it almost impossible to hear.

At the door Kenny and Caleb paused to let their eyes adjust to the dim light. "Find a corner," Caleb whispered. "Out of the way."

Kenny crept to a rough bench against a wall, far from the entrance. They sat there.

Caleb bent close to Kenny's ear. "Look in the far corner," he said.

Kenny saw three men around a table. He recognized one of them as the man who had given him the message to deliver, the one Caleb called Esek Ormsbee.

"That is Seagrave with him," Caleb said.

Kenny asked, "Who's the other?"

"Arial Peake," said Caleb. "Slave merchants, all of them, in the African trade."

Kenny studied the group. The man nearest Ormsbee was a fair-headed, clean-shaven man, who despite the heat wore a blue coat edged with lace. The other was not so richly dressed.

Caleb went on. "I believe they are meeting because of you," he said.

"What do you mean?" Kenny said, surprised by the notion that he had any connection with what he was seeing. As far as he was concerned all this was Caleb's life, not his.

Caleb nodded. "It was that note you delivered."

Kenny felt like objecting but Caleb nudged his foot. "Come on," he whispered, "we need to get closer if we are going to learn anything."

Reluctantly, Kenny pushed himself up and began to work his way through the crowd in search of a place they could listen from without being too conspicuous. As they went by the group he was able to overhear their talk.

"He's past time," one of the men was saying.

"He'll come," Ormsbee said. "He gave his word."

"With plans, I hope," said another.

Kenny found a likely place to hide, a partially open door which led into what appeared to be a small, dark room. When his questioning look toward Caleb brought a nod, he slipped behind the door. Caleb followed.

Kenny couldn't make out the dank space. "What is this?' he whispered.

"A holding pen."

"Holding what?"

"Slaves," Caleb replied, his voice low. "There should be another door in the back. Might be useful. You stay here and listen. I'll look for it."

Kenny knelt by the partly open door. By leaning forward he was able to observe the men at the table.

"But are the rumors true?" one asked.

"They are," said Ormsbee. "Mr. Brown and his people intend to present a petition to the Assembly next week. They'll be calling for full enforcement of the trading acts."

"We would be ruined!"

They began discussing custom agents, the Congress, laws passed, laws broken, as well as men whose names meant nothing to Kenny.

As Caleb rejoined him, Kenny asked, "What are they talking about?"

Caleb listened briefly. "Keeping the slave trade open," he said.

Kenny said, "I thought it was forbidden."

Caleb gave a snort. "No one enforces the laws."

Kenny heard Ormsbee say, "He's here." There was a scraping of chairs as the three men got to their feet.

Curious as to who the new arrival might be, Kenny edged further forward and peeked out. It was Pardon Willinghast.

* * *

Kenny's heart gave a lurch. Then as fear swept over him, he felt an overwhelming desire to run. And in fact, he says, he had turned from the door when Caleb's hand clamped down hard on his shoulder, making it impossible to move. Caleb's grip — far from being reassuring — brought him yet more fear. It began to dawn on Kenny that he had no control over what was happening.

"Good evening, gentlemen," Kenny heard Willinghast say in his familiar, soft voice. "I am sorry to be so late. Please, sit down."

The men resumed their places.

"Mr. Ormsbee," Willinghast went on, "I don't know what you have told these men."

"Only about Mr. Brown and his petition," Ormsbee informed him.

"Then I can be brief," said Willinghast. "Gentlemen, it will be no good talking to Mr. Brown or his people. They have no intention of listening to the voices of moderation. We have made it clear to the public that a cessation of the African trade will bring great harm to this state.

"But gentlemen, Mr. Moses Brown and his faction merely front for others. The blacks themselves are the true agitators in this affair. If we can bring *them* to silence, Brown and his people must back away. Our task is to set the spark aflame.

"Perhaps you noticed those men and boys sitting outside. I arranged for them to be there. They work the ships, and they are greatly upset by what might happen. Why, sirs, they might lose their livelihoods.

"If these men," Willinghast continued, "were to proceed to Olney Lane, and do no more than make their views, which are our views, known there — that they wish the African trade to continue — I don't doubt but that something would come of it. Something that would force the general population to see this matter from our point of view. Moreover, such a proceeding would inform the blacks that if they pursue the matter further they are in grave danger. All these men need is a word from me."

Kenny, who had been concentrating as hard as he could, now turned toward Caleb.

"Caleb?" he called, his voice as loud as he dared make it. There was no answer. Kenny stood up and peered into the dark. "Caleb!" he called again.

Still there was no reply.

Alarmed, Kenny moved away from the door and groped about until he found the room's back door. It was open. He looked outside. The area was deserted.

Not sure which way to turn, thinking he had made some mistake, Kenny retreated back to the holding room, and the door behind which he had been listening. From there he stole a look into the tavern.

The original three men were working their way through the crowd toward the front door. But Willinghast remained at the table. The man was looking directly at him.

Kenny could only stare back. Willinghast gestured toward one of the empty chairs, offering a seat.

At that point Kenny whirled around and frantically sought the rear door, only to find it closed.

He tried to push it open. It wouldn't come. He rushed back to the inside door. Now it was wide open, but Willinghast himself was blocking the way.

"Please," said the man. "It is impossible for you to leave. Besides, it would be much better if we engaged in a conversation." So saying he stepped out of the room.

Not knowing what else to do, Kenny followed. The moment he did, he was grabbed from behind by a man who had been hiding off to the side. One hand clapped over Kenny's mouth, preventing him from crying out.

"His pockets," Kenny heard Willinghast bark. The man began to search him with his other hand. In a moment he flipped Kenny's Dodgers key chain onto the table.

The old man snatched it up and looked at it. With a satisfied grunt of approval he turned to the man holding Kenny. "Let him go," he ordered. The man stepped back.

"Do not worry," Willinghast said to Kenny, again in his soft voice. "I shall not hurt you. Quite the contrary. But for your own safety you must come along with me. We shall talk."

Kenny was barely able to think. He found

himself following Willinghast out of the tavern, and it was only then that he noticed the man was limping.

Willinghast led him to the water's edge, a quiet place save for the occasional slap of the water against the wharf posts. There he stopped, turned, and looked at Kenny with obvious satisfaction.

Kenny stared at him, desperately trying to make some sense of what was happening. "What are you?" he said.

"Like your slave friend," said Willinghast with a show of ease, "in your time I am a memory. But here, like him, I am real. And my business is to trade in blacks — buy them on the Africk Coast, bring them to Cuba or the Carolinas, sell them. It is a profitable affair and I fully intend it to continue. And you have your role to play in that."

"What role?"

Willinghast held up a hand. "All in good time."

"You knew about Caleb from the start, didn't you?" Kenny said.

"I did."

"Where is he?"

"No doubt trying to prevent what is going to happen from happening."

"What's going to happen?"

Willinghast smiled good-naturedly. "So many questions! You heard what I told my friends."

"Did Caleb know about your plan?"

Willinghast shook his head. "Only vaguely. He would not have come to the tavern if he had known. And I presume that he ran off when he heard my plans. You see," he added with a smile, "he is doing exactly what I want him to do."

"What's that?"

"You shall see."

"I don't want to be a part of this," Kenny insisted.

Willinghast smiled. "My good boy, you already *are* a part of it."

Kenny shook his head. "I'll go back," he insisted.

"Back?" said Willinghast. "Where?"

"To my time."

By way of replying, Willinghast reached into his pocket and held up Kenny's key chain. Despite its cheapness and the dark of the night, the chain glittered like a jewel. You will remain as long as I hold this," he announced.

"What do you mean?" Kenny cried.

"Kenny Huldorf, hear me well. Alter yourself, hurt yourself, lose something you have carried with you, and you become something different. Become something different and you cut yourself off from your own time. You shall become a ghost, haunting *this* time!

"But continue to do as I want you to do — fulfill *my* memory — and you shall have your chain back. Then and only then will you be able to return to your time." Willinghast carefully placed the key chain back in his pocket. "But not until then."

Dumbfounded, Kenny could ask only, "What's going to happen?"

Willinghast smiled sternly. "In time," he said. "In time . . ." So saying he brushed passed Kenny.

"But what do you want me to do!" Kenny shouted after him.

Instead of answering, the old man disappeared into the dark.

Kenny felt as though a spell had been lifted. At once he bolted away up the hill toward Benefit Street. From there he raced to Sheldon and his own house. Still clinging to hope, he headed for the back door, found it, and pounded up to the attic. What he found, however, was the dreary room that proved he was still in the past.

Close to tears he sat down on the top step, trying to grasp what was happening. At that moment all he could understand was that he was caught between contending memories — Caleb's and Willinghast's — of August 17, 1800. Each was trying to make the past what *he* wanted — with Kenny's help.

He knew what Caleb wanted. To change things so as to get free. And he grasped that Willinghast wanted him to help keep them as they had been.

Kenny didn't have any doubts about what *he* wanted: to help Caleb. But Caleb had abandoned him, was always so suspicious and doubting. Why couldn't they be friends? It wasn't he who had treated Caleb badly. Why did Caleb keep suggesting he had?

As for Willinghast, Kenny hated him. He knew that too. The old man's words — that he, Kenny, might become trapped here, a ghost from the future — had frightened him deeply. But then why hadn't Willinghast told him what he wanted him to do? And — Kenny recalled with a start — what did Willinghast mean by saying he was *already* doing his part? All along he had believed he'd been helping Caleb.

As Kenny remembers it, only then did he consider the idea that he'd already done what *Willinghast* had wanted him to do, that *nothing* he'd done had been of his own will. Perhaps he had only set a trap for Caleb.

Kenny stood up. He had to find Caleb and tell him what he knew.

But no sooner did he decide to do that than he realized he had no idea where Caleb was.

In an attempt to calm himself Kenny tried to go over what had happened in the tavern. All he could guess was that while he had been concentrating on Willinghast's words to the three men, Caleb had overheard something important to him.

Kenny tried to reconstruct what was said. It took a while, but when he did, the one clue he could dredge up was a place called Olney Lane.

But how, he suddenly asked himself, was he to know that *this* was the right thing to do? He remembered Willinghast's warning. What if he did the *wrong* thing? It might mean he would never get back to his own time! Or perhaps going to Caleb was exactly what Willinghast wanted him to do.

"I shouldn't have come," Kenny whispered to himself out loud, aware suddenly of his own trembling. "I never should have."

But he knew he had to try and find Caleb to warn him. He had to.

* * *

Kenny returned to the street. The first person to come by was an elderly man carrying a lantern. Kenny approached him.

"Please, sir," he said, "can you tell me where Olney Lane is?"

Startled, the man stopped and lifted his lamp to examine Kenny. "What do you want there?" he demanded.

"I'm looking for someone."

The man continued to scrutinize his face.

"Please," Kenny implored. "It's urgent."

Turning, the man said, "That street." He was pointing to Benefit. "Go to the left and then to the end — about a mile. A little beyond, up the hill, that's Olney Lane. But," he concluded in a fearful whisper, "you shouldn't be showing your face there."

"Why?"

The man looked about as if afraid of being overheard. "Some sailors are said to be going that way. They won't want to see the likes of you unless you plan to mix in. Keep out of it." The old man hurried off.

Kenny watched him go. He even considered running after him and pouring out all that was happening to him. The next moment he realized that no one would believe him. No one.

He set off in search of Caleb.

CHAPTER SEVEN

It didn't take long for Kenny to reach the foot of Olney Lane. All he could make out through the darkness was a row of small houses extending single file up a hill. It was too dark to count their number. And what he could see of them suggested they were small structures, nothing like the ones he had grown used to on Benefit Street.

Here and there he could see the pointed gleam of a candle set behind drawn shutters. The more he looked the more Kenny realized that people were hiding.

A rumble toward the south made him turn and look back. It sounded like distant thunder. The air, hot and heavy, seemed thicker; he was sweating, as much from tension as heat, when he started again toward the hill.

"Who's there?" he heard.

Startled, Kenny peered into the darkness, trying to see who had called.

"Who is it?" came the voice again.

"Caleb?" he asked.

The figure came a little more into the open. Now Kenny was able to see that it was Caleb. He moved toward him but stopped short when he saw that Caleb held something in his hands.

"What is that?"

"A musket."

Kenny tried to see the gun through the dark. Then he remembered what had happened before in the tavern. A spurt of anger went through him. "Where did you go?" he demanded. "You shouldn't have left me like that."

"I couldn't take the chance that they would see me and hold me," Caleb explained. "I had to warn the people here. Did Willinghast say more about what they are going to do?"

"I don't know how much you heard," said Kenny. "He was talking about sending sailors up here."

"That I heard," Caleb said. "Did you see anyone on the road?"

"No."

"They'll come making remarks and insults, wanting someone to react. They won't stop until they are answered, either. That is all the excuse they need." He patted his gun. "I will give them a reaction."

Kenny gazed back the way he had come, wishing he knew how to say everything that he now knew. "Maybe that's what Willinghast wants you to do," he finally said.

"I don't care what he wants," Caleb said. Then, as if checking himself, he added, "The storm could break. That might hold them off. People like that, they can't abide weather."

They sat down next to each other, their eyes on the Providence Road. Now and again flashes of lightning followed by low rumbles of thunder broke against the southern sky. Kenny wished the storm would hurry.

For a while neither of the boys spoke. Then Kenny said, "Caleb, Pardon Willinghast set this whole thing up."

"The mob? I know."

"No, more than that. You left too soon. He found me and dragged me out." Even in the dark, Kenny was aware of Caleb's eyes. "He seemed to know," Kenny continued, "that I was in that room listening all the time. Caleb, he even knew you were there, knew you escaped. And . . ." He faltered.

"What?" Caleb said.

Kenny sighed. "I know him from the twenty-first century."

Caleb swore under his breath. "Are you sure?"

"That was him outside my window the other night."

"I should have guessed," Caleb murmured.

"He said everything that's happened is his doing. Is he right?" When Caleb didn't answer he asked again, "Is it?"

"It better not be."

Kenny needed a moment to grasp Caleb's meaning. It made his heart sink. "Aren't you sure?" he said.

Caleb's silence was the answer Kenny dreaded. "Caleb," he said, unnerved by the uncertainty, "Willinghast said if I hurt myself, or change anything, even lose anything it means I'll stay here."

"How can that be?"

"I don't know, but that's why he took my key chain. Unless I do what he wants he won't give it back. And that means I can't return."

"What's he want you to do?"

"Wouldn't say."

After a moment Caleb got to his feet.

Kenny peered anxiously through the dark at him. "That's why I came. It thought you should know what he told me."

"Here I thought you came because you wanted to help me," Caleb said.

"I do," Kenny said quickly.

"Then don't go quitting now," said Caleb.

Kenny felt trapped again. "Caleb, do you think that your murderer will be among the ones coming?"

"Probably."

"Have an idea who it is yet?"

Caleb shook his head. "It could be any of them."

"How are you going to know who it is?"

"I will know. Anyway . . ." Caleb stopped talking.

"What is it?" Kenny whispered, instinctively lowering his voice.

"Listen."

Kenny caught the sound of voices singing loudly, raucously, one voice vying with another to be louder than the next, as if they wanted to be heard from a distance.

"Drunk," Caleb said with contempt. "They have no courage to come without that." He shifted the musket across his chest.

Kenny stood too.

They saw the torches first, two of them, flames sputtering angrily in the wind. Then lanterns, piercing the night with hot intensity.

Looking down from the hill Kenny tried to count how many there were. His first guess was thirteen. His second was twenty.

He turned to Caleb. In the reflected light of the torches, Kenny saw the muscles in his neck throb with tension. "I think we should leave," he whispered.

"I'm not going to let them just march up here," Caleb said.

"Caleb," Kenny pleaded, edging away, "I'm scared."

"Don't you think I am!" Caleb shot back. He was standing firm in the middle of the road, gun in hand.

The men below had stopped their singing. Now they were milling about some twenty yards from where Caleb stood, whispering among themselves. It was clear they were undecided about what to do. It was equally clear that they had not noticed Caleb.

"We can get closer," Kenny heard one of them say.

"No one's going to do anything," agreed another.

"Look at the place. All closed up. Asleep in their beds."

The remark brought laughter, not natural but forced, as if the men needed it to remind themselves that they were all there, that they were having a good time.

"Scared silly of us," chimed in another.

"Right," came another voice. "Come on. Let's get it done before the storm."

Their confidence renewed, the mob came up the hill a little further. Kenny could see them more easily now. At least three looked like kids his own age. Some of the men seemed to be carrying what looked like pikes. A few held clubs. The way some moved — swaggering, stumbling — it seemed certain that Caleb had guessed right. A good number had been drinking.

"Long live slavery!" one of them suddenly shouted.

"No free niggers!" joined in another.

Kenny felt ill. The hot breeze about him seethed with the drunken violence of the men.

There was a pause as the mob waited to see if any response would come from the house nearby. When there was none, the mob grew bolder, more rowdy. They moved up the hill a little further, still unaware of the boys only a few yards away.

Lifting their pikes and clubs into the air, a few of the men cheered. "Huzzah to slavery!"

Caleb took a few steps closer, Kenny, watching anxiously, drew deeper into the shadows. He knew that Caleb was frightened — knew he would be crazy not to be — but was trying to hide it.

The mob continued to shout and jostle forward, staying within their own circle of light as if it were some protective shield.

It was the men at the front of the mob who saw Caleb first. They stopped clumsily and, holding their lanterns high, leaned into the dark. Those behind bumped into the ones in front, cursing and shouting.

Even as the men gaped at him, Caleb held his ground. The men became still. Kenny heard the wind stir the leaves of the trees. It came like weeping.

One of the mob found his voice.

"Nigger, you're blocking the way."

"This is a free road," came another taunt.

Caleb stayed still.

"Right," another man jeered. "We're just here for a stroll."

Caleb took a step toward them. "Clear out," he suddenly shouted. "Clear out!" Kenny heard the great strain in his voice.

"Hey, it's just a boy," called someone. The discovery appeared to reassure the mob.

"Don't tell us to clear out!" someone else cried.

"We've every right to be here."

There was a chorus of approval. Kenny could see that some of the men were trying to look past Caleb, to see if anyone else was on the road.

"There's not going to be any trouble," Caleb announced. "Go home."

To the south lightning flashed. The thunder drew closer. Kenny began praying that the storm would break, anything to prevent what he felt was certain to happen.

A voice shouted, "Get that weapon away from the nigger. Go on! Get it away!" There were more advice givers. But no takers.

It was then that someone bent over to the ground, scrabbled about, stood up. Kenny saw that he had a rock in his hand. The next moment it flew through the air and landed near Caleb. Caught by surprise, Caleb jumped back.

His awkward retreat broke the tension in the crowd. Some of the men laughed. Almost immediately others began to gather rocks and hurl them. Caleb, on the defensive, stepped further away, but not fast or far enough. One of the rocks struck him on the shoulder. Another smashed into the side of his head. Reeling, he put a hand to his bleeding face, then stumbled and fell, losing his musket.

Kenny remembers running from the shadow and grabbing Caleb by the arm in hopes of pulling him up and away. Caleb tried to shake Kenny off.

Kenny's sudden appearance made the men pause. They looked to see if there were others hiding in the darkness.

"There are too many of them," Kenny cried to Caleb. "We have to get out of here!"

When the men saw no one else following, they once more started to advance. More rocks landed all around the boys.

Caleb jerked himself free from Kenny. "Keep out of the way!" he screamed. His eyes were large with fear. He gathered up his musket and clutched it nervously.

One of the men broke from the crowd and flung his torch toward Caleb. It streaked through the air like a meteor. Other men made a rush at him, shouting, swinging their pikes. With Kenny at his side, Caleb turned at last, and retreated about thirty yards up the hill.

The men veered toward the nearest house.

Howling and jeering, they attacked the small building with their pikes.

Lights began to appear inside. There were cries of terror. The men were tearing at the house with clubs, pulling out planks, smashing doors. Then they moved to a second.

The sight was too much for Caleb. He lurched forward, stopped, lifted the musket to his shoulder, aimed into the mob, and fired.

The sharp report was almost instantly followed by a scream. One of the mob fell to the ground. Around him, men and boys froze, first looking toward Caleb, then at their comrade on the ground. It was clear, even from where Kenny stood, that the man was dead.

Caleb tried to reload his gun, but he was not fast enough. The men set upon him with howls.

Caleb turned, tripped, dropped the musket, tried to retrieve it. But the men were too close. Kenny, desperate to pull him away, reached for him. This time Caleb came.

Breathless, the two stopped at the top of the hill to look back. The men were no longer following. The first of the houses they had attacked was in flames. People could be seen fleeing. The air was filled with their cries.

Caleb, stock still, stared at the scene below. Blood, and tears of rage, ran down his face.

At that moment the storm broke, bringing sudden, torrential rain. Lightning lit the skies. Thunderclaps burst repeatedly overhead.

"Come on!" Kenny urged, taking hold of Caleb's arm. "We can't stay here."

Caleb, his mouth twisted in pain, shook free. "I can't leave," he said. "I can't."

The rain was making the roadway a cascading stream.

Kenny tried to look downhill to see what was

happening. Beneath the deluge, torches and lanterns began to sputter and go out. Even the burning house was smoldering.

"Look," Kenny cried. "They're backing off!"

The mob had begun to retreat. The dead man was being carried into the dark. The storm poured down.

"There's nothing more you can do!" Kenny shouted.

Caleb said, "I have to get the gun!"

"It won't be there!" Kenny insisted, still shouting. "They'll have taken it." He put a hand on Caleb's arm. Caleb did not resist. "Come on!" Kenny cried.

Caleb turned and allowed Kenny to lead him away.

CHAPTER EIGHT

They traveled by lightning, for without it Kenny could see nothing in the blackness, could feel nothing but the rain and sloshing mud underfoot. But as the lightning lessened he had to turn to Caleb and shout, "I don't know where we are!"

Caleb looked at Kenny without comprehension. Only then did Kenny remember that when he'd first seen Caleb, he'd seemed hard of hearing in one ear. Now he knew why. It explained the scar too. He moved to Caleb's other side, and repeated himself.

That time Caleb heard. He stood up straighter and looked around. "We're near Ferry Road," he said. "We can take it. It runs behind the town."

"Where are we going?"

"To Sheldon Street."

"This way?" asked Kenny, pointing into the darkness.

Caleb nodded. "I'll tell you when to turn."

Kenny looked at him. "You're hurt a lot, aren't you?"

"My ear," Caleb said.

In his chest, Kenny felt a great swell of grief and regret. "Caleb," he cried out, "I never knew things like that happened. I didn't. Really. You were so brave. . . ."

"I thought you were going to help," Caleb said.

"I wanted to. . . ." Kenny began. He could almost feel the intensity of Caleb's gaze and was stung by the words. "But, Caleb, if I got hurt, or . . ." seeing Caleb's pain he didn't know what to say.

"Or what?"

"I told you. If something happened to me Willinghast said I'd have to stay. Here."

"Yes, you . . ." said Caleb and he turned away. Kenny saw his shoulders twitch.

"Come on," Kenny said, putting his arm around Caleb. "We'll get you to your room."

*   *   *

The back door to the house was open. With Caleb insisting upon leading the way, they went inside. He found candles, struck a spark, lit one of them, and held it before them as they trudged upstairs.

As they climbed, Kenny glanced back over his shoulder. To his surprise he saw that only one of them was casting a shadow. He could not determine which one.

Caleb stuck the candle upright on the floor of the small room, then lay down on a straw-stuffed mattress.

The thin taper, with its small, flickering flame, filled the space with a sickly light. Though they were home, the boys felt little comfort. Caleb was exhausted, Kenny shivering. He saw what looked like a blanket in one corner and he put it over Caleb, who accepted it with a thankful nod.

Kenny took a place on the floor, back against the wall, and kept his eyes on Caleb. Caleb lay quietly on his back, staring up at the ceiling. Now and again he put his hand to the side of his face and sighed.

Remembering the missing shadow on the stairwell, Kenny held his hand near the candle flame and glanced across the tiny room. It was he who cast no shadow. Only then — as he remembers it — did Kenny realize that he was as much a ghost in Caleb's world as Caleb had been in his. *He was haunting Caleb.*

"Caleb," he said, "maybe your being there tonight kept things from getting worse."

"Maybe."

"And you're alive, you know. Don't forget that. You weren't killed. It didn't happen."

"I wasn't meant to be killed there," Caleb said. "Someone will come."

"Here?"

"It's what happened before."

"All of it?"

Caleb nodded. Then he said, "I killed one of them. You saw that, didn't you?"

Kenny, who didn't want to be reminded, reluctantly said, "Yes."

"They can't accept that. They will have to do something. You will see. Someone will be chosen to come here to make sure my murder is done."

"I can stop him."

Caleb grunted, "With what?"

"What about Mr. Brown?"

"Who?"

112

"That man I saw by the market. The one who was going to offer the petition to the Assembly. Moses Brown. He's on your side, isn't he? Wouldn't he help?"

After a moment, Caleb said, "I don't know."

"I could try getting him, couldn't I?"

Caleb's hand twitched under the blanket. He shook his head. "Please do not go."

"Why?"

"They are watching, waiting for you to leave. Once you do they will come for me."

"How can you be so sure?"

Caleb sighed. "How often do I have to tell you, this is the way it was."

Kenny, battered by feelings of helplessness, tried to think. He pushed himself up.

"Where are you going?" Caleb called.

"To check the street." Kenny went into the main room and, on his knees, looked out one of the low windows. It was dark but he was still sure the street was deserted.

Returning to Caleb, he said, "No one's there. Where does this Mr. Brown live?"

"Too far."

"Caleb," Kenny insisted, "I have to get someone. I can go and get back fast."

Caleb shook his head. "Please, do not."

Kenny fingered the door, trying to decide what was best. As he did his hand caught on a nail. Irritated, he twisted it and tried to pull it out. It wouldn't give. But it did give him an idea.

"Hey!" he exclaimed. "You can lock the door. From the inside."

Caleb looked around. "How?" he asked.

"With this nail," Kenny suggested. "See, it'll twist onto this other one, but not come off. As soon as I leave — I am going to try to find someone — you can lock the door behind me. You can do that, can't you? And I promise, I won't be gone for more than thirty minutes. Twenty if you like. Honest, you need some help."

"You won't find anyone."

Ignoring him, Kenny pulled the door shut, twisted the nails together, pushed against it. The door held fast. "See?" he said. "It works."

Caleb heaved himself up, came over, and tried the door. It held. Kenny saw that he was still bleeding and very weak. He felt more determined than ever to get some help.

"Satisfied?" he asked Caleb. Caleb didn't respond. "You need help," insisted Kenny. "But if

114

I see anyone on the street who even looks suspicious, I won't go further. I promise."

"Just hurry," Caleb said, resigned. He lay down again on the mattress, then rolled over onto his side, face to the wall.

For a moment Kenny stood undecided, looking at Caleb's back. He saw no blood stain. That was enough to convince him that there was still time to get help.

"I'm going," he announced.

Once he pushed it closed, Kenny called through the door, "I'm out!" He stood in the attic, listening.

In moments he heard Caleb inside the room moving toward the door. Then he heard his efforts to twist the nails together into a lock. Kenny rattled the door. Again it held. Satisfied that Caleb was safe, he went down the steps and then outside.

The rain had stopped. Overhead, a few stars had begun to emerge. The glow of the moon could be seen behind scudding clouds. Kenny inhaled deeply. The air smelled fresh and clean.

He looked up and down the street, cautiously searching for signs of movement. Wet spots on the sidewalk gleamed. He saw nothing else, but still he felt nervous. He wished he had his key chain.

Just as he began to run toward Benefit he heard a cry, "Kenny Huldorf!"

The words reverberated as loudly as any thunderclap he'd heard that night. Kenny stopped and turned so quickly he almost fell.

A man was standing in the middle of the street. He was clothed completely in black, from the three-cornered hat that covered his brow to the cape that draped his shoulders and flowed to his knees.

Pardon Willinghast.

"Boy!" he called. "Come here!"

There seemed to be no resisting that voice. His heart hammering, Kenny approached the man. He wished he had listened to Caleb and had never gone from the house.

Willinghast stood with one hand lifted. From it something glittered in the moonlight — Kenny's key chain.

"I still have it," said Willinghast.

Kenny was too frightened to reply.

"All I need do," Willinghast continued, "is fling it away." He made a gesture of doing so. "Or

116

destroy it." He folded his fingers around the chain. The glitter was snuffed out. "If I did, you would remain here. Alone forever. Haunting a world not your own.

"Or," he went on, dangling the chain again, "you can return to your world. Your home. Your life." Teasingly, Willinghast seemed to hold it out as if making an offer.

Kenny could not keep himself from reaching for the chain — but Willinghast withdrew his hand with a smile.

"I told you at the tavern that to get it back you would have to do something for me. It is time to tell you what that something is."

Kenny tried to draw himself up. He wasn't very successful. He felt completely cowed. "What is it?" he stammered.

Willinghast reached under his cape and produced a double-barreled pistol. Alarmed, Kenny stepped back. Willinghast held the gun out before him.

He said, "I want you to kill that slave up there."

Kenny felt ice close around his heart.

"'Find my murderer,' he said to you. And you did. What you didn't know was that you were looking for yourself. I arranged that just as I have arranged it before."

"Who was it the first time?"

"Me."

"But the newspaper said it was a suicide!"

"The newspapers . . ." Willinghast said with scorn. "The first time they had it right. 'Slave killed following disturbance on Olney Lane.' No one cared then.

"But Caleb could not accept that. He insists upon his freedom. So he haunts that house hoping to change what was. Do you think you are the first to have lived in that house? The first to be haunted? The first to reach this point? No. He is persistent. But, I assure you, he always fails. For even as his memory reasserts itself, he brings me back too. Am I not part of his memory too? And I am there to block him. After all, I am a historian, a guardian of memory, memories which *I* choose and shape. When I arrange things as I want them the newspaper story also changes. You read the revised version."

Kenny shook his head.

"Yes," Willinghast went on, "you, like all the others have done, will kill him in that room with this pistol."

"This gun is loaded and primed," Willinghast said. "Both barrels. You merely draw back the locks, pull one of the two triggers, and it will be done. In case you bungle the first, the second barrel will give you a second shot.

"When that is done, when I have seen him laid out with his blood on the floor, I shall return your charm to you.

"Take it, lock the door from the inside, place the pistol by him, then return to your own time. No one shall know. Ever. How could they?

"Once again Caleb's death will be reported as a suicide, brought on by remorse over the vicious shooting of the sailor this evening, as well as the violence visited upon his own people. In one sense, the report will be accurate. He has brought death upon himself.

"Of course, the right people will understand that it was *not* suicide. But the person who did it — you — will be beyond all reach. And time."

"I won't do it," Kenny managed to blurt out. "I won't."

"Oh, as with most of the others, you will have remorse," said Willinghast. "You will try to find a way out. But I believe you will do it. And then! . . . you will forget what you did."

119

"Why?" demanded Kenny.

"To save yourself," Willinghast said coolly.

With an almost ceremonial gesture he placed the pistol on the ground. "There," he said. "Think of it as a fair exchange. His life for yours. Not a jot more. Or less. But fail me, and I swear by all the powers I command, you will stay here. I shall give you until dawn."

So saying, Willinghast turned and limped down the street, leaving Kenny alone.

Recovering his senses, Kenny sprang to the pistol and picked it up. "I won't do it!" he screamed. "I won't!"

But the street was empty. Willinghast had blended with the shadows. Kenny looked down at his hand. He was holding the pistol.

CHAPTER NINE

Kenny rapped softly on the door. "Caleb," he said. "Caleb?" He could hear movement inside. "It's me, Kenny."

"Just a moment," came Caleb's voice. Kenny listened as the nails were twisted around. Caleb pushed at the door cautiously. When he saw it was Kenny he swung it out the rest of the way. "You took longer than you said you would."

"Sorry," said Kenny, slipping in.

"Did you find anyone?"

"I tried one house which still had a candle burning," Kenny replied. "They wouldn't answer."

"It's much too late. Must be close to dawn."

"Is your face hurting?"

"I believe I have a fever," Caleb returned. "I feel awful weak." He went back to his mattress and lay down.

Kenny resumed his place on the floor, back against the wall. By the candlelight he stole a frightened look at Caleb. He could see at a glance how weak he was. All the same he said, "I think you should leave."

"Leave?"

"Run away. Somewhere."

Caleb struggled to prop himself up on one elbow. "What are you talking about?"

"There must be someplace you could go. To be free."

Caleb stared hard at Kenny, then shook his head. Finally he said, "What happened?"

Kenny couldn't look up.

"Something happened," Caleb insisted. "I can tell. Did you see someone?"

Kenny said nothing.

"Who was it?" Caleb demanded.

After a moment, Kenny spoke. His voice was so tight he could hardly talk. "I . . . I found your murderer."

Caleb jerked himself up completely. "What?"

"You heard me," Kenny whispered. A sudden wave of anger toward Caleb came over him. It was as if Caleb was the cause of his own misery. "I found your murderer."

"On the street?"

Kenny nodded.

"Who is it?"

Kenny said nothing.

"Tell me!" Caleb demanded. "Who is it this time?"

"'Me," Kenny said.

The candle fluttered. Caleb stared at Kenny with horror-filled eyes. "What do you mean?" he managed.

Slowly, painfully, Kenny told Caleb all that had happened when he went outside. How Willinghast had been there. What he had said. The demand. The threat. At last he took from his pocket the pistol he'd been given and placed it on the floor between them. After that he remained silent, looking down, ashamed before Caleb's eyes.

Caleb said, "Did you really try to find someone afterwards?"

"Caleb . . ."

"You are lying," said Caleb. "You went out. You met Willinghast and you came right back here. Isn't that the truth?"

After a moment, Kenny said, "Yes."

"Then at least," said Caleb, his voice even, "I know what happened."

"Caleb . . ."

"What?"

"I don't know what to do."

"I see. . . ."

Convulsively, Kenny kicked at the gun. It skidded over near the mattress. "I won't do it," he said, as much to himself as to Caleb. He looked up, willing to face Caleb squarely for the first time since he had come back to the house. "I won't."

Caleb returned his look. "You do not mean that."

"I do!" cried Kenny, tears starting down his face.

"Liar!" Caleb snapped.

Kenny shrank away.

For a long time Caleb gazed at him. Then he struggled to his feet and crept into the other room. There he knelt down to look out one of the windows. "Come here," he called.

Kenny, sniffling, pulled himself together and followed. Across the street, framed in a doorway, a man was standing. They couldn't see his features, but Kenny had no doubts. "Willinghast," he said.

Back in the small room, they sat looking at each other. Kenny felt a great swelling of pain within his chest. "Caleb," he said, "when we began you said all of this was your memory. But it's his memory too. And he's more powerful."

Caleb shook his head. "Making it his memory makes it easier for you, does it not?" he said. "Makes it seem like you are not in control."

"I'm not."

"People," said Caleb scornfully, "abide by the memories they choose."

"I don't want to kill you!" Kenny shouted at him.

"Then do not do it," Caleb returned softly.

"But what will happen to *me*?" Kenny cried. "If I save you *I* have to stop living!"

"You are alive. And free."

"I'm not," Kenny returned forcefully. "I'm a ghost here. The way you were a ghost in my time. You were trapped in that room. You needed me to get back here to your time. Now he won't let me back to mine unless I kill you. Caleb, don't you see what he's done? He's trapped us both! Each of us. *We are haunting each other.*"

"And I say to you, do not let me be killed again," Caleb said.

"Just tell me what to do," pleaded Kenny with rising desperation, "and I'll do it."

"Change things."

"I don't know how!"

"'Do you really not know?"

"No!"

"Kill Willinghast."

Kenny was dumbfounded. "What do you mean?"

"By destroying him we make the memory ours." Caleb rushed on before Kenny could object. "You said he told you he would come to this door once my blood was on the floor."

Kenny nodded.

"He can have that," Caleb said.

"I will put it there. I'll even lie on it the way he wants. Then, when he comes, you can be out there." He pointed beyond the room. "With that." He nodded toward the pistol. "Then the rest will be up to you."

"Me?"

"It can't be me."

"Why?"

"Because you are the only one who can really get away."

Feeling sick to his stomach, Kenny pressed his hands together.

"Afterward," Caleb continued, "we will bring him in here and take your charm from his pocket. I will make my escape while you close yourself in this room. Then you will escape to your own time."

"Where will you go?"

"I am not sure yet."

"Will you be free?"

"I will try."

Kenny swallowed hard, shook his head. "I don't know if I can."

"There is no other choice," Caleb pressed. "Not for us. The way he has it, it's you or me. Do you want to give him that?"

Kenny shook his head. "And your blood? How will you get that?" he asked, trying to quell the tremor he felt.

Caleb put his hand to his cut face. "If I press here," he said, "it will bleed again. I will rub some on my back, and lie down. Then you will fire one shot. Willinghast will think . . ."

". . . I've shot you," said Kenny, hearing his own words as though from a distance. "He'll come up. See you lying there. Think you're dead. . . ."

"He will give you your chain," Caleb continued, "and you will shoot him."

"Caleb," Kenny said in anguish, "don't you think we're only doing what he wants us to do? Maybe it's just another one of his traps."

Caleb nodded. "You are afraid."

"Yes," Kenny admitted.

"Do you think I am not?" Caleb asked. After a moment he got up, left the small room, and looked again out a window. After gazing at the sky he came back. "He is still there. Do you know any better way?"

"No."

"How much time do we have?" Caleb asked.

"He said till dawn."

"Well then?"

Kenny closed his eyes, opened them. Caleb was waiting for his answer. Then he nodded yes.

Immediately, Caleb took off his shirt and folded it so that a square of the back was exposed. He handed it to Kenny who began to rub it gently against the side of Caleb's face.

"Harder," Caleb insisted, and winced with pain.

The wound broke open. Kenny felt ill.

"Go on," said Caleb, "get the shirt in it."

Reluctantly, Kenny dabbed at the blood until a large red stain was marked on the shirt. Kenny gave it back to Caleb who put it on. Kenny was startled at how much the shirt looked like it had when Caleb first appeared.

Caleb lay down on the floor.

"Caleb!" Kenny cried, his voice choked.

"What?"

"This is all too much like it was. I keep thinking it's some trick of his. Like we're only setting this up the way he wants us to. How can we be sure it'll work? You might die."

"I did die," Caleb returned.

"The first time?"

"Every time."

"You said — before — 'Who is it this time?' *Was* it always the same?" asked Kenny. "Getting someone to help you, going up on the hill, trying to stop the mob . . . that happened before?"

"That is my memory."

"It was Willinghast who killed you the first time," Kenny said slowly. "Since then you keep trying to find someone to help you get free."

Caleb nodded.

"And they've always betrayed you."

"Someone has."

129

The full sense of Caleb's history rose up before Kenny. It seemed horrible beyond measure. But he thought of something else. "Caleb," he said, "if you do get free from here, it still might happen again, at another time. Another place! Is that right? What I'm asking is," Kenny said, "if this works, is it really going to change anything?"

"You are wasting time," Caleb said harshly.

"Tell me!" cried Kenny.

"Just let me get past this one," Caleb finally said. "Now go on, shoot off the first barrel. There is only a little time left. We've got to make it look right for Willinghast."

Brought up short by Caleb's urgency, Kenny retreated to the doorway. From there he looked back into the small room. Caleb was lying face down on the floor, his shirt stained with blood. By his side the candle, reduced to almost nothing, burned with a tiny blue flame. Its feeble light made the room seem hollow.

Kenny lifted the pistol. He realized then how right Willinghast has been: it would be so easy to kill Caleb. He could do it without anyone knowing. He'd get back to his own time, free and safe.

With a violent shake of his head, Kenny chased the idea away. That was wrong, he told himself, *wrong.* But his right hand was shaking so, he had to use his left to help control it.

Steady at least, he drew back the lock, then pulled the trigger. The pistol fired. The candle flame twitched violently, almost went out, recovered.

In the closeness of the attic the explosion made his ears feel as if they'd burst. His eyes smarted with smoke.

For a fleeting moment Kenny thought he had shot Caleb. "Caleb?" he called, more frightened than ever before.

"I am here," Caleb replied. He had sat up again. "Go on out there and wait for him."

But Kenny, not wanting to be alone with his thoughts, lingered by the door. Caleb, though small on the floor, cast a large shadow against the low wall.

Kenny, stalling, asked, "Want me to put out the candle?"

Caleb shook his head. "I feel better with it there." He lay down, clearly exhausted.

Kenny hesitated. "Caleb," he whispered.

"What?"

"I don't think I could be more scared," he said.

"Same for me," Caleb said.

Kenny turned to leave.

"Kenny!" Caleb called huskily.

"What?"

"Come here."

Kenny went back into the doorway. Caleb had rolled over. He was holding out a hand. Their fingers touched.

Caleb said, "You are my friend."

*　　*　　*

Feeling his way, Kenny moved as far as he could from the small room, to a position near the top of the attic steps. There he listened, wondering why Willinghast had not already arrived. When the notion occurred to him that the man might not come, his heart began to pound. He looked toward the room. All he could make out was the faint flickering pulse of the candle stub.

"Caleb?" he called.

There was no answer. Without checking, Kenny felt certain that Caleb, worn out by all that had happened, had fallen asleep.

At that moment Kenny realized that everything was *exactly* as it must have been before. As

Willinghast wanted it to be. He felt fate closing down around him. And around Caleb. Once again thoughts of killing Caleb formed in his mind. He felt sick.

Like a fever wave, a hatred of Willinghast moved through him so strongly it was difficult to breathe. If only he could be sure he *could* destroy the man. Yet, the idea of his killing someone . . . Kenny shuddered.

He tried to pull himself together, thinking again that it was all only memory.

Is memory real? he asked. *Can you kill a memory? Change it?*

From the bottom of the steps there came the sound of a door opening. Kenny held his breath.

Shaking, Kenny moved farther away from the top of the steps. In an attempt to hide it from view, he placed the pistol behind his back. Then he turned to the stairwell. Someone was coming up.

Gradually Pardon Willinghast emerged from below. The sight reminded Kenny of how Caleb had risen from the floor — like a ghost. Top of the head. The face obscured by dark. The shoulders. The rest of the body, until he was standing in the attic.

After pausing briefly at the top of the steps, Willinghast started to cross the room. Unexpectedly he stopped. As if he knew all the time where Kenny would be standing, he turned and said, "I will determine if you have done it."

Kenny could only nod dumbly and make a small gesture indicating the room at the other end of the attic.

Willinghast walked to the small room and stood on its threshold. He looked in, his back to Kenny.

Hand trembling, Kenny drew the pistol from behind his back. He managed to lift it but only by steadying his one hand with the other. He aimed the gun at Willinghast.

Casually, almost indifferently, Willinghast turned toward him. He saw the gun. Smiled. "He's only asleep."

The words froze Kenny. His arm faltered. The gun lowered.

"I knew you wouldn't do it," Willinghast said. "That you'd need some encouragement. Very well. You have done what I wanted you to do. So far. For which I thank you. Now, the rest."

Willinghast drew a watch from beneath his cape. He consulted it gravely. "It's almost dawn."

Kenny stared at him, but he didn't move.

Willinghast's voice rose in impatience. "Do as I bid you. Afterward you'll go into the room — with your charm — and lock the door from the inside. You *will* escape into your time. A perfect crime, so perfect even you will forget what you have done. Your memory will be your alibi. I promise, you will have no remorse. Do nothing and you will stay here. But quickly now, if you are going to save yourself."

Drawn by Willinghast's voice, Kenny moved forward. He could feel the weight of the pistol in his hand.

"Close," coaxed Willinghast, moving a step closer himself. "There's only one shot left. It must not be wasted."

Kenny stopped and stared into the room. By the light of the small candle flame, sputtering in its last moments, he saw the sleeping body of Caleb.

"He will never know what happened," Willinghast pressed. "Ever. Draw back the hammer. Hurry!"

As if the action were something separate from himself, Kenny heard the click of the pistol's hammer pulled back into place.

With his free hand Willinghast held up Kenny's chain. "Look," he called.

Kenny turned. He could see the shimmering key chain swing from Willinghast's hand. He looked against the wall. The shadow of the chain looked like a hangman's noose.

"Fool!" cried Willinghast. "Do it now! As it was meant to be. Save yourself, Kenneth Huldorf."

Trembling, Kenny lifted his pistol.

"There," said Willinghast, his voice straining. "It will happen as it was meant to happen. He means nothing to you!" Like a promise he held out the chain.

Kenny pulled the trigger.

*   *   *

Kenny lay in his bed, caught between wakefulness and sleep. Gradually he came to full consciousness. Once he realized he was in his own attic, he swung his feet to the floor and tore into the small room. There he looked at the floor. The stain was gone.

Kenny actually ran to the Historical Library, hurling himself up the steps to the newspaper room. Breathless, he spoke to the woman who was behind the desk, the same one who had helped him before.

"Can I," he gasped, "see the film I looked at when I came the other day? August 27, 1800."

It took only a short time for him to find what he was looking for. It was in the issue of the August 27, 1800 paper. There was no reference to Caleb's death. But there was another notice. It read:

UNFORTUNATE DEATH OF PARDON WILLINGHAST

The unfortunate death of Pardon Willinghast, merchant and trader, has been reported. Mr. Willinghast was found in an upper room of 15 Sheldon Street. From the circumstances attending his death, it appeared that he took his own life, insofar as a pistol was found by his side, and the door was locked from the inside. It is not known why he was in the building. A slave, Caleb, owned by Daniel Stillwell, has escaped from the same building. He is being searched.

Kenny returned the spool of microfilm to the woman.

As she took it, she said, "When you came last time, you said you got permission from a Mr. Willinghast. I checked but — I'm sorry — no one by that name works here."

It was Kenny who took me to the old ceme-
tery, the one just north of the modern city of
Providence.

"I want you to see this," he said.

It was an unkempt place. The stones were pit-
ted and stood at crazy angles. Here and there
strange carvings were to be seen. More than one
stone had toppled completely over. But Kenny
knew exactly where he was going.

"There," he said, pointing.

I looked at the stone he indicated. I could see
instantly that it was an old grave. It sat quite
alone, fenced in, the only one in that particular
area. On the grave, this is what I read:

PARDON WILLINGHAST
Born 1704
Died in Providence August 18, 1800
Aged 96
Taken in Violence by his own Hand
R.I.P.

"It was me," said Kenny, holding on to my
arm as if he might fall. "I was the hand. Back
then. I don't know what happened to Caleb. He
left. And I stayed in the room with . . ." he paused

and looked at the gravestone "... Willinghast. I took the chain."

I realized then that he was clutching the chain in his fist.

"I fell asleep," Kenny continued, "and woke ... here. Now."

I looked at him. His face was so very pale. And as he gazed up at me, I could see how deeply troubled he was.

"I keep thinking about Caleb," he said quietly. "You know, what happened to him. I only helped him get out of *that* room. I keep thinking he's in some other house, some other room, trying to change another memory. That's why I go walking around a lot. There are so many old houses here in Providence. I don't know how to find him." Kenny's look had become imploring. "Do you think he's free yet?" he cried. "I mean, really free?"

May 1988
Providence, R.I.